WRONGFUL

To Bathsheba — with profound gratitude & joy! Lee

LEE UPTON

Sagging
Meniscus

Set in Mrs Eaves with LᴬTEX.

ISBN: 978-1-963846-21-8 (paperback)
ISBN: 978-1-963846-22-5 (ebook)
Library of Congress Control Number: 2024946169

Sagging Meniscus Press
Montclair, New Jersey
saggingmeniscus.com

For you, the rightful reader

Contents

WRONGFUL

PART ONE

⊬ CHAPTER ONE

S OMEWHERE UNDER the massive, plasticized sheet spread on the hillside above the lake, tons of garbage, liquefying, were poised to slide. Not that the women on the shore were thinking about the landfill. They stood on loose gravel, the oldest propping herself against a boulder. The lake, flecked with silver, dimmed as clouds shifted the light.

"Do you think she came here to the lake?" the novelist Luisa Chaudette asked the biographer Tama Squires. Midges feasted on the women's humid breath. It was warm for mid-October.

"What I know is this," Tama Squires said, with an air of authority that Luisa Chaudette already assumed was customary. "Mira Wallacz probably couldn't help herself when it comes to any body of water. Water is a muse for many of us. Maybe she went too far. A cramp? Out too far and in too deep." She squirmed against the boulder as she pondered the disappearance of Mira Wallacz. Incredible that such a seemingly dull woman could put out a full-size novel each year with the regularity of production practiced by breeding animals, such as the rabbits Mira wrote about with weirdly undying interest in her books for children. It was a trend, wasn't it? Novelists writing children's books while also composing the most lurid fairy tales for adults. They were all doing it—every novelist interested in easy money. She turned again to

Luisa Chaudette. "Maybe she actually was murdered, and we're the means to discover the truth? Any minute her body will come floating by."

Luisa looked out toward the lake before she said, "If that happened you'd sell more books, wouldn't you? If you manage to write her biography."

Tama laughed, clearly not offended. "I don't know why you'd ever think anything at all like that. I'm not a materialistic person in the least."

Luisa stepped back. "I didn't say you yourself murdered her."

Tama laughed again. "We're being so morbid. Probably she wasn't murdered. Although she might enjoy the notoriety." What, after all, was the festival except a way for Mira Wallacz to confirm and extend her reign over her readers and capture more attention? She had paid for most of the three-day festival from which she vanished, even though she was scheduled to be in attendance the entire stretch.

Then again, it was possible that the biographer herself was the reason for Mira's disappearance. Maybe Mira remembered that little prank Tama played on her and was exacting vengeance by vanishing.

Luisa brushed away another cloud of midges. "I saw those Instagram posts of her in her pool. The one where she's wearing basically nothing except a rosary. Swimming and drinking don't mix well."

"I'm not convinced it's her in some of those photos."

"Photoshopped?"

"I don't know. Maybe another person altogether. The photos are so blurry."

"Not that blurry. Her jaw—I'd know it anywhere."

Tama said, "You would? Maybe I should be interviewing you for Mira's biography."

Approaching across the gravel came a woman, long dark hair brushed with red highlights, the same woman Tama snubbed at breakfast. She appeared at the biographer's elbow and reintroduced herself as Yolanda. "I can hear you from yards away," she said. "You think she was swimming drunk? I've never seen her drunk. I mean, she'll have something in hand sometimes. Basically on the order of a Shirley Temple, you know? She likes those new nonalcoholic fermented drinks. Cheating for alcoholics. We were childhood friends—and stayed friends."

Gravel slithered under Tama's feet. She really should head back to her hotel room in the conference center. Standing too long hurt her joints. Still, maybe this Yolanda person knew something useful. "You were her friend? So you must have been told she wrote those novels before anyone else knew?"

Yolanda turned away from Tama. "No, she didn't tell me, although I should have been told. When I think back . . . Santi—she was in the book club—she owned one of those early novels years ago. Seeing that book in Santi's carryall—peeking out—I caught the look on Mira's face. The pride. Sheepish pride. I didn't follow up on that, so I was left in the dark. Anyway, Mira was disappearing all the time even back then. One of her tricks. To get us talking about her before we knew she wrote anything, except for those children's books. We knew about those. You think she might have been murdered? I guess just because she wrote about murderers in those obscene books doesn't necessarily mean she's the victim of one, Nevertheless—"

"How can you be sure?" Tama interrupted, swiping at the air in front of her nose. "Some genetic coding could be speaking through her art. Were any of her relatives violent? Maybe you would know about that? You said you've known her for years. You knew her family too? Maybe I should interview you? I'm her biographer."

Yolanda nodded. "Authorized?"

"Not yet. But I'm sure she'll agree."

"I can tell you this," Yolanda said, "her entire family going back generations—they were just about all born illiterate."

"That explains everything," Tama said, winking at Luisa who had been listening to both women. "You're awfully quiet, Luisa. Why do you think Mira writes the way she does, with so much erotic material that's romanticized? Maybe it's not porno to you given the salacious stuff you write, but my god, look at who's here at the festival. Pretty much only people who identify as women."

"I don't understand," Luisa said, frowning and shifting her weight from her left leg to her right.

"What Mira writes only works for women. It's not at all like men's pornography. It's—"

"More subtle?" Luisa suggested.

"God no. It's just more—aquatic. Fluid. It intimates—"

Yolanda interrupted with a cough. "I probably know Mira more than anybody here, and I don't think she considers her work pornographic, although it is. She doesn't understand her readers, and so it's hard for her to care about them. Even the readers of her kiddie books. Well, you know. Children are so needy. I myself love her children's books. I think she's the best children's book author of her generation. The most edgy, anyway. When you look closely, her bunnies appear like they're sneering, you know? Or like they're smoking and the cigarettes have been airbrushed out."

"Are you suggesting in a roundabout way that Mira smokes?" Tama asked. "I didn't know that. That's an interesting detail. For anyone doing research. You know what they say about research?

You can lose your life in research. I ought to know. My dangerous profession. Ha!"

Yolanda raised her voice. "I didn't actually say that Mira smokes!"

"Well, I wish she smoked so we could follow the trail of smoke," Tama said. "She really hasn't let anyone know where she is. We're all here for her. It's rude of her to disappear."

All three women looked to the woods beyond the lake. Oaks and pines and a smudginess at the horizon.

Yolanda shrugged. "Part of me has always wondered: How can she not be murdered? Eventually? When I found out she wrote the novels I told her, Honey, you're going to get murdered someday as sure as the sun comes up shining. She was poking the bear a lot even back then with the children's books. I always felt there was a message for adults in those rabbits. Like: watch out, people, here I come, Mira Wallacz, and those rabbits are going to make your kids hate you because you're not as nice as rabbits, as cute as rabbits, as willing as rabbits to entertain the imagination, you know? If she's murdered—I'm not saying she's murdered—I do know she did all the prep, stirred a lot of unconscious anger."

As Yolanda spoke, Luisa contemplated how it's a terrible thing to recognize that someone you once condescended to, someone you felt embarrassed to be seen with, achieves what you cannot: not only popularity among readers but nods of admiration from professional critics. Luisa picked up a pebble "You're wrong about her," she said to the two other women. "She's loved. Very loved. She's not stirring up anger—at all. Years ago I met with my publisher, Ottoman's. Mira was there that day in the office. She was leaning against a wall and wearing a blue and white dress—flowers on it—and looking a little lost, you know? She asked me to lunch and we went to The Prufet, and I was hoping no one saw me with her. I know, I know—how ridiculous. I actually felt superior to her. I was the one writing genre-busting fiction, and I thought she was only drawing pictures of dopy animals. She must have read my mind. First off, she told me she would pick up the check. Then she told me we could count on our privacy. No one would recognize her, she said. She asked me about the subject of my debut novel and didn't act scandalized. You know how it was in those days. I thought no one had anything over on me, that Philip Roth—this must seem like ancient history—had liberated all of us for decades, regardless of gender. I thought Kathy Acker prepared the way too. What an idiot I was! When the reviews came in for my novel they might as well have sent in a team to feel me up for a witch's teat. Oh, but Mira—when she talked about those critics to me—the worst one from *The Times*—she unleashed obscenities at more length and with more inventive formulations than I'd ever heard and I'd already heard plenty. In the next few years we had maybe a total of five lunches, and I never saw that side of her come out again, I suspect, because I was so busy talking about myself." Luisa grinned and the two women stared at her. "What I mean is, she could make you love her, she really could."

The publisher Inger Delft, yards away on the bank, listened to the women without joining in or turning toward them. She had her own opinions, which she never would voice aloud, opinions that were ready to burst into words if she weren't cautious. She had unwavering opinions, that's for sure. For instance, such as how, if she had been Mira's publisher, she wouldn't have let one single sentence go by. No, Mira's sentences. Never giving off light, not even the dimmest dying battery crackle. Those books Mira wrote for adults—they were for children, really. And the books she wrote for children, they weren't for anybody. I could have saved her infinite pain, Inger imagined. Or should I say, Inger told herself, I could have saved her readers pain. And now Mira had disappeared from the conference, Emily Dickinson-ing it all. Holing away, skipping panel presentations she was supposed to respond to. So where was she? She's not dead. That wouldn't follow the logic of the plots she foists on readers. No woman is ever harmed in her novels, except for the first cadaver as an inciting incident. Always, no matter what, a happy ending for women. That's how much she manipulates her readers.

Could vanishing be a marketing ploy? Abler Books makes Mira Wallacz their cash cow and so now to juice up new interest she's disappeared? She funds a festival—a celebration of her work and influence—much of it masturbatory—and on the second day she gets people worked up, wondering where she is, who she's with, why she's run away. The worst attendees traipse down to this dishpan dirty lake and moan about her, like she's stuck in a crab pool and they're ready to consult the runes—as in that Viking movie from my childhood, a childhood absolutely wonderful because her children's books weren't in it, and as a consequence I wasn't subjected to the sort of contrivances that would have created in any healthy child an aversion to rabbits. In book after book those rabbits make stew. Stew! So no one puts them in a stew because they're already on to the game! Like she's writing a survivalist guide for rodents.

Enough: the day is young. Time for Inger to look over her notes for her first presentation. What wisdom could she impart? Should she say: I don't know what I can tell you that will give anyone hope about the state of publishing. Should she lie? Pretend optimism? Tell the audience that if I myself ever wrote a book, say a book about this festival, I'd write about a gorgeous sorceress who makes the bland and tolerable disappear. Even if I added rabbits I'd sprinkle them with bad attitudes so that little girls don't think their natural ruthlessness is anything to be ashamed of . . .

Was that a torn garbage bag floating in the lake? She really needed to get her eyes checked. She blinked, shook her head, blinked again. The turtle was aiming toward her, its long neck stretching. Like a snake half hiding under a heavy backpack. Maybe people regularly fed turtles in the lake. If that turtle expected to get something from her it was a bit of an idiot.

Before Inger turned around to head back to the conference center a plaintive voice rang out: "Why doesn't anyone know where she is?"

No one had noticed Geneva Finch standing, silent as a rabbit, beside one of the spindly pines. The girl even looked like a rabbit, Inger thought. A feral rabbit—stringy and dingy-haired, soiled, like she popped out of a burrow.

The girl repeated herself, took one step closer.

Tama cleared her throat and answered. "It's a no-show for the time being more than a disappearance. Mira likes deception, that's what I'm betting. Don't fret, honey. She'll turn up." After all, it wasn't like wanking Agatha Christie's famous disappearance. No husband's mistress is involved, no elaborate cover story developed, no string of obvious lies.

Luisa nodded in the girl's direction and raised her voice. "We're all concerned, but I'm sure Mira's not trying to deceive—"

Tama laughed. "Oh, people want to be deceived. They pay for it. What else is fiction for? Inger, what are you doing over there? I bet you agree!"

Inger spoke for the first time. "She'll turn up. It would be a loss to literature if we didn't hear from her again." To anyone listening her voice sounded like a wish more than a prediction.

⊷ CHAPTER TWO

ENEVA FINCH SLUNK AWAY and up the ridge toward the conference center. She was embarrassed by her outburst. What
made her think she had the right to shout out to those
women? Disappointment. Enough disappointment to make her
heart ache.

To come all this way and find Mira Wallacz missing. After taking two buses and walking part of the way when the bus couldn't
drop her off directly at the center. The conference center, she had
learned, was new—otherwise the bus route would have wound all
the way to the entrance.

The second bus was the worst. Geneva watched the land pass
from the window to her right and tried to avoid being annoyed by
the teenager tossing a ball in the seat ahead of her. The ball tossed
higher, the boy's shoulders wriggling. He must have heard her sigh
because he twisted around, his head bobbing over the seat, his eyes
daring her, the whites visible at the lower rim. She remembered,
wincing, her last years of high school. Bird calls, bird caws.

The boy's head was almost at her chest. So close she could smell
his sour breath—like vegetables left in the refrigerator too long.
Something sweet too. Strawberry gum. She knew how she had to
behave: motionless. The way you would with a dangerous animal.

At long last, her stop. Halfway down the aisle she remembered her backpack on the seat and hustled to retrieve it. The boy stuck out his leg. She hopped over it. As she hurried to the front of the bus, the boy's gaze was still so affixed to her that her shoulders pinched.

The directions were on the flyer in her backpack. She didn't really need them, she'd memorized them.

A pickup whipped by. That was the most for traffic until a cement mixer chugged over the rise. The woods on each side of the road gave off a spicy, dusty smell. It was tempting to leave the road and walk into the woods, the sun flaring golden through the heaving leaves. A sudden mentholated chill in the otherwise humid air, the trees dropping leaves and the leaves spinning in front of her face. Golden. Some trees had more to drop, and sooner.

The straps of her backpack dug into her shoulders. And then right before making her way to the conference center up the slope she found herself on the shore of a lake and heard those women talk about Mira Wallacz—saying that the author had vanished. In the tone of their voices, no matter what they said, under their words was something else: they were glad Mira Wallacz was gone. Geneva heard it all. Their voices: it was like she was still smelling that boy's breath on the bus.

Yesterday she registered for the conference at the reduced student price because she was taking a class at the college even though she could hardly afford it, but she managed. She would always manage. Except for paying for the overnight rate at the conference hotel. She would sleep in the woods if she had to.

Maybe those women were wrong and Mira Wallacz already returned? What if the novelist was standing near the center's entrance, like at the head of a receiving line? Geneva wouldn't know what to say, wouldn't know where to look. Would gawp. Just imagining such an encounter, she stumbled, plunging forward, nearly falling flat.

Once she recovered her footing, she breathed deeply to reclaim herself. Drawing in her breath again she smelled plastic burning. Maybe she'd been smelling it for minutes but had been too engrossed in listening to those women to register anything more. She wondered if the smell rose from the lake, if the water churned with chemicals. Maybe the lake was dangerous, maybe Mira Wallacz had taken a swim and lost consciousness from toxins. Someone should drag the lake for a body. Or were those women just playing around with hurtful ideas? You didn't fantasize about someone's death in such a casual way if you cared about them.

Geneva turned to look down the slope at the lake, glimmering in the October light. The women on the shore were breaking off from one another. She took another shaky breath. She wanted to get inside the center before any of the women caught up to her.

She stopped at the sight of a stone mask half-shrouded with leaves on one of the center's entrance pillars. She'd seen a mask like this before: the Green Man, the guardian, if she remembered correctly, of growth and decay. The stone looked new, something acquired online through one of those shops that specializes in faking medieval artifacts. A duplicate mask was attached to the pillar to her left. The smile on each face didn't convey humor, more like airy indifference.

In the lobby Geneva wound her way between white couches and artificial trees in mammoth pots. In her peripheral vision she saw stacks of Mira Wallacz's books on a long table. She recognized one of her favorites, *Tea Dialing*. The figure on the cover looked like Geneva's mother in her high school picture: big haired, dreamy eyed.

Just ahead: a table with a registration sign. At the table sat an officious-looking woman already staring at Geneva. The woman probably had a daughter in a high-ranking college, a daughter who wore clean, fresh-smelling clothes.

She imagined what the woman saw: Geneva's hair already oily-looking even though she washed it last night, and the spottiness of her skin. Her jeans that were clean but never appeared clean. She didn't look at the woman's eyes again but wouldn't forget them. That was something she learned from reading Mira Wallacz and her descriptions of characters' eyes. Eyes tell as much as voices. You look into someone's eyes and it's hard to hide, but it's hard for the other person to hide too.

The woman answered Geneva's question and watched her step back, hot-faced, until the woman whispered, "There's something."

On the bottom bunk lay a brown suitcase and on the table next to it: a hairnet like a balled up spiderweb. Faucet sounds. Out from the bathroom came a white-haired woman, so feeble looking and thin that Geneva sat down on the bottom bunk out of sympathetic exhaustion.

"Hope you don't mind me," the woman said in a voice that sounded younger than her face looked.

"I hope you don't mind me," Geneva answered, emphasizing "me."

After snatching up her hair net the woman said, "You're not paying anything either are you? I hope not. Every one of these festivals has charity beds and we're it. You have to game the system if you're on a reduced income, you know? You don't mind having an old lady roommate?"

"I'm glad you're my roommate," Geneva said, not lying. She wouldn't have to impress this woman, and maybe the woman would do all the talking.

"You probably haven't heard about the problem," Geneva's roommate said, announcing that the featured speaker, Mira Wallacz, was missing.

"I heard some people talking about it down by the lake."

If Mira Wallacz wasn't located soon, the woman said, the police would have to be informed. As of now, it was too early to file a missing person's report. Suspicions would have been aroused in more quarters if Mira Wallacz hadn't already made a habit of being mysterious at other events at other places and setting off on her own and disappointing her readers and for such a long time writing under a pen name, not letting anyone get to know her until her identity was revealed by her agent. "Do you think she's just an attention hog?" the woman asked. Her eyes were very bright, very blue.

"She doesn't need attention," Geneva countered, feeling the need to defend her favorite author. "My mom read me her books for children when I was little and then later I heard about her dirty books and read them all." She regretted saying "dirty books." Her roommate might not even know about those books, might be here only because of the sad rabbit books. Anyway, the books weren't all that dirty.

"I've never read any of her kiddie books," the woman said. "That sort of stuff—I wouldn't have liked that as a kid. The dirty books . . . I'd recognize dirt, real dirt. They're fantasy books, aren't they?"

Geneva tossed her backpack on the upper bunk. She didn't think the old woman would steal anything, plus what was there to steal?

The woman wasn't done talking. "So many people find her books relaxing, somewhat like Sudoku. All is right with the world. Everyone in their little boxes."

Geneva couldn't tell if the woman thought that was a good thing.

Luisa Chaudette waited to head back to the center until Tama, Yolanda, and that sullen person—Inger something—drifted away from the lake. She needed to go on a little walk, while she could— that is, before Mira appeared, for certainly Mira couldn't be gone for long—since late yesterday afternoon, wasn't it? Mira had to show up at some point. And Luisa really should get a walk in be- cause she felt more sluggish than ever. Being around Tama Squires, that could make anyone take a vow to improve their health. Tama needed to prop herself against a rock for most of the time they were at the lake shore. Let that not be my fate, Luisa cautioned herself.

The path thinned, brambles clotting on both sides of the path. She was soon amid sumac and black-eyed Susans and purple- headed thistles ranging higher than her head. The sun's warmth on her shoulders bore down. Strangely enough, it was relaxing to feel a bit lost. Maybe getting lost was exactly what Mira had wanted and that's why no one could find her. Mira could be stumbling along the path at any minute.

The urge to confess. What Luisa almost did just minutes ago: confess to those women, Tama and Yolanda. And then that strange, straggler of a girl asked her question, startling them, and the mo- ment was gone. Thank god. Luisa's confession would have done nothing for anyone. Might have even harmed her terribly. Really, she was saved by that girl's question. Saved from the impulse to destroy her own life. When her life was already pretty much de- stroyed.

Luisa Chaudette could have told the other women that she thought she saw Mira Wallacz last night right there in the lake. While taking an after-dinner walk, Luisa heard splashing and imagined that the person in the water was a stranger thoroughly enjoying herself. How exciting to swim at night, to put all your fears away, and to let yourself splashily careen around under the stars. Her next thought: I know who that is. That's Mira Wallacz, probably having a marvelous time in the lake for the past half hour, while the rest of us ate that inedible dinner with those terrifyingly tiny shrimp glued into the risotto. That's just like Mira Wallacz—relishing her solitude and swimming alone, needing no one, communing with nature and her own soul. Mira was that self-sufficient, that cold-hearted. During yesterday afternoon's first session Luisa had performed terribly on a panel when talking about her own work and Mira Wallacz's influence. How indifferent Mira had looked as she sat in one of the high-backed upholstered chairs, hardly listening, her eyes closed. Maybe she was actually sleeping throughout the entire panel presentation! Mira Wallacz was an icon while Luisa was someone to ignore, at best to tolerate. Luisa's talk was so blubbery and inconsequential, too self-deprecating. At one moment of particularly high tension she couldn't see the page she was reading from and her mind did this mirroring thing and she saw herself, but not as a human woman. She saw a giant walrus with flat pancake hands. Thank god she snapped back into herself and read again from her paper. During the question and answer session what possessed her to talk herself down all the more, admit and elaborate on her failures, tell everyone (even Mira Wallacz!) that she was an eighth-rater. What did that even mean? But look at her life from the past five years, won't you? Luisa practically had to sell her novels out of the trunk of her car, like Jacqueline Susann before she got famous. And she couldn't get past writing about the same sort of character: an unsuccessful woman eaten alive by envy. Whereas Mira Wallacz had written for herself at least multiple meaningful lives in novel after successful novel. Her characters found justice and love. So much so that Luisa couldn't stop herself from wondering: why should Mira Wallacz have more life? And Mira's childhood wounds—whatever they were, she'd closed her wounds with her novels, hadn't she? If she ever had one single wound. The best revenge in those novels; living comfortably, eating especially well . . . How couldn't Luisa feel—not jealousy but something worse, like Mira's existence erased her own?

All these thoughts passed through Luisa Chaudette's mind as she watched the person in the water—and at last noticed that Mira's arms were either flailing or waving. Maybe she was drowning. The way the body in the water was turning about, and then the head going under. And it was all so quiet suddenly. Like watching a silent movie.

As she walked among thistles Luisa reprimanded herself about the previous night: I didn't do anything. I didn't call out to Mira or turn and run for help or . . . Can you go to prison for that?

And oh God, forgive me for what I did when I saw Mira drowning—I turned away and ran up the ridge.

Luisa could imagine the look of revulsion that would have passed over the other women's faces if she confessed.

But then, she reminded herself, after first hurtling away from the lake and up the ridge she turned around and headed back to the shore, prepared to jump into the lake and save Mira Wallacz.

When she had reached the gravel beach she yelled god knows what across the water until a stranger came stomping out, spraying lake water and cursing. What's wrong with you? the woman shouted. And Luisa muttered, Everything. Everything's wrong with me.

The swimmer turned out to be the daughter of the main chef at the conference hotel's restaurant.

And now, today, by an odd coincidence, Mira Wallacz couldn't be found—had disappeared, exactly as if Luisa's awful thoughts made her vanish. As if the woman in the lake had been Mira after all and Luisa let her die. It was horrible, that thought. Luisa was glad she never had to confess how far she'd fallen from goodness, how sinister her thoughts had become, as if they weren't her thoughts as all, but contagious, something she caught at the festival.

Mira Wallacz. Those adult novels will die out first, Luisa imagined. The children's books, though, those might have lodged into too many little minds. Yes, all those books that Mira wrote—someday the landfills will be packed with them.

Seeing that woman in the lake, a woman she thought was Mira Wallacz . . . Until she realized she was disappointed that the swimmer she imagined drowning wasn't the novelist after all, Luisa Chaudette hadn't known she hated Mira Wallacz. Even now, shame heating her face, she hoped there wasn't a search party.

She circled back on her meandering walk and there, ahead of her, loomed the conference center's upper parking lot, right where it should be. She was never lost, although lost in her thoughts. At least Luisa Chaudette herself wasn't the sort of person who abandons her readers.

And the fuller truth about yesterday: she hadn't seriously considered jumping into the lake to save the person she thought was Mira Wallacz. No, but she did return to the lake on almost a trot.

⊁ CHAPTER THREE

ACK IN HER ROOM at the conference center, Tama Squires considered her chances of wheedling an interview with Mira Wallacz. If Mira turned up. You just had to hope she wouldn't be pigheaded and decide to ditch all her commitments. Frankly, although it was interesting to entertain the idea, it was grotesque that people thought Mira might be dead just because she hadn't shown up since late yesterday afternoon. As if someone like Mira Wallacz didn't have the right to give herself a breather.

No doubt people were only saying she was dead because people like horror and mystery. It makes them feel important and alive. Why else would anyone attend funerals? Besides, Mira was too vain to die, too self-protective. Mira knew, always, what she was doing. It was just that no one else could figure out why she was doing what she did. Her persona for years had to be a calculated charade. When her agent began giving interviews, sucking up temporary fame for herself, she was asked if she wasn't betraying her client by revealing Mira's identity. To which the agent replied, "Mira did a good job of betraying us all."

Tama plugged in the filthy-looking coffee maker to heat some water. Thank god she'd brought her own canister of her favorite grind. She needed coffee for the next sessions, though maybe she'd skip those. And if she got too buzzed from the caffeine, that was okay. She needed plenty of energy to fantasize more profitably about Mira's disappearance, which surely must be temporary.

Tama just had to play her cards right and hope Mira would allow herself to be questioned at length. Maybe she would even authorize the biography. What a coup that would be. Provided Mira was more interesting than Tama suspected. Well, Mira would make her interesting. You can't be sued for speculating, if you're crafty.

Possibly Mira was meeting a lover? Wouldn't that be fun to write about, if it was someone famous? But what if she didn't show up and let them all molder around waiting for her. Ugh. And then— who knows what Tama should do? Maybe take another nice stroll down to the lake again before it got dark? Nothing strenuous. She really had to get healthy, get her heart rate up more often and prove she was good to go. Plus, strolling would give her time for thinking without the clutter of other minds, like the mind belonging to her wife Lizette, who was set to arrive before long. It wasn't easy to do your own thinking around Lizette—she swallowed so much energy. So many people do. Like earlier when that midlist fiction writer Luisa Chaudette showed up at lakeside and that annoying townie Yolanda Eng had to keep interrupting. Well, what were festivals for? Inevitably you meet people and probably that constitutes "networking." The term should have fallen out of use decades ago. It makes you think of flounder struggling in a fishing net and gasping. Well, nets did work. You just had to lower yourself.

Mira Wallacz's agent, Stephanie Binks, popped in and out of sessions, unsure if anyone recognized her. In the early days, like everybody else, she didn't know Mira's identity—their business had been conducted by mail and only later through the internet. Why Mira wanted to be unknown was a mystery. Mira should never have thought for an instant that she could have the level of anonymity of Elena Ferrante—even if back then she didn't know someone calling herself Elena Ferrante existed. No, anonymity was simply arrogance. It takes an enormous ego and just as enormous resources and a non-US passport to keep an identity hidden. And so it was that, eventually, Mira's anonymity had to be dropped. At the right time. And profitably. By Stephanie Binks. Who led readers to reality: to the real Mira Wallacz. And now people at the festival thought Mira Wallacz was missing. They thought she might be dead. Even the featured writers thought as much. Amazing how macabre writers could be about other writers.

Macabre and puritanical. There are always purists who think revealing a writer's identity amounts to a desecration of the dead, especially if the writer is still alive. Imagine that. But let me tell you something, Stephanie Binks would very much like to repeat to certain people: Mira never told me not to reveal who she was. Never wrung out any obligations, other than for me to do my best to get manuscripts to the right publisher. Look at the acknowledgements page of every novel written by Mira Wallacz and see who's thanked. Stephanie Binks. Always.

The first time Stephanie Binks encountered Mira's writing: a standard letter requesting representation arrived in a manila folder with a post office box number for return address. Stephanie skimmed the letter and read the writing sample and found herself laughing. Remember those Ken Russell films from decades ago? Over the top *Lair of the White Worm* stuff? The plot was on that level. Bawdy in a soft-core way and unpredictable and implausible. Nevertheless, Stephanie Binks took a chance. For the sheer fun of it. What was life about if you didn't place yourself in a daring position, do what no one else thought likely to garner success? The only interested publisher was operating out of a basement. A lucky choice for the publisher given that the book soon sold to actual readers. The magic of word of mouth. After that, manuscripts came every year to Stephanie, the only return address that post office box. Back then, Mira used a pen name: Audrey Plinth, a name like something invented by a British dowager in support stockings, and all business was conducted through that same post office box. Mira would never agree to meet with Stephanie, never detail her own life, only admitting to using the account owned by a local parish for depositing funds. So Stephanie Binks hatched a plan. She sent an envelope, enormous, red, and knew roughly when it should arrive. She staked out the post office, conveniently in the same town as the one where Stephanie's youngest aunt lived. (As a consequence her aunt got more visits from her niece than she hoped for.) At last, after three tries in two months, right before Stephanie was about to give up waiting in her car, she witnessed a frizzy-haired woman in green ballet slippers loping out of the post office clutching one of those outrageous red envelopes. And she knew then: knew who the woman was who kept her identity as a novelist secret. It was that author of children's books, Mira Wallacz. They had met years ago at a luncheon. Mira Wallacz, the quiet, rather forgettable author of inane children's books. Who would have thought the same woman wrote provocative novels that readers consumed like boxed chocolates? Now you couldn't escape knowing who Mira Wallacz was. And her Instagram following in recent years: fabulous. And readers clamored for more and were not disappointed, so far. At least for now—if Mira didn't choose to slow down. And Stephanie Binks knew about every one of Mira's choices. After all, Mira told Stephanie just about everything. Her hopes and plans and the plots of her novels. Sometimes it was a real trial. Like Mira thought Stephanie had none of her own resources, no plot of her own that was hers to keep. When the truth was: Mira's plots actually belonged to Stephanie Binks, Mira's dedicated agent. She suggested character arcs all too often for Mira, who relied on her.

A nice run around the perimeter of the lake—a good time for it soon. Stephanie's muscles were all knotted up. Or maybe not. The mood had to strike her. She was only yards from the entrance of the conference center when her right foot sank into muck. The moist ground sucked in more, grasping her heel. Groaning, she pulled her foot out and scuffed the bottom of her shoe in the grass. It made her think of a potential plot for Mira, if Mira would get her ass in gear. In the plot—as usual, Stephanie was always feeding Mira her best ideas—a woman gets sucked into a giant cavern under the earth . . .

She was maneuvering between potted orange mums on the entrance steps to the conference center when she heard her name. "Stephanie, up to your old tricks?"

Misery. Hideous Inger Delft, hurrying to catch up to her. Inger had never accepted any manuscripts from Stephanie's clients, including Mira's first efforts, despite cajoling. And now Inger couldn't help but resent the agent's success.

"Your cash cow has disappeared," Inger Delft cried out. "You know where?"

Could this person be more annoying? Inger should resent herself, not Stephanie, for missing the chance to corral a cash cow for herself.

Stephanie Binks hurried on, taking the center's steps two at time, pushing open the windowed door, only stopping when she was in the lobby and couldn't remember where the elevators were, to the right or the left.

Inger Delft, close behind her already, repeated herself. "Where's your cash cow?"

How marvelous it would be to punch Inger in the throat. Instead, Stephanie said, in her calmest, most professional voice, "Inger, you should know that Mira is a very private person."

"So you're not worried."

"I never worry about Mira. There's never anything to worry about. I make sure of that."

"Maybe you should worry. I hope being her agent isn't more trouble than she's worth."

"I don't have any trouble with Mira." The agent nearly spat her client's name. "I have to hurry. A phone call. It's important."

"That's what people like you always say," Inger Delft muttered, the muscles of her jaw tightening. "You're predictable, you know that?"

Standing behind a couch in the lounge, and not sure what to do with herself, Geneva Finch watched Stephanie Binks hustle off, with Inger not far behind. How was it that Mira Wallacz drew such terrible people to the festival, people like Inger Delft, with her sly insinuations? Geneva didn't know yet what Stephanie Binks's or Inger Delft's connection was to Mira Wallacz —except that money was involved. A cash cow. Geneva imagined a black and white cow with enormous swaying udders spurting nickels.

Disappointing. So disappointing. The cynical, begrudging tone of these people, their lack of idealism. The way they subtly or not so subtly let you know they felt superior to Mira Wallacz although they pretended otherwise. Why did these people dislike and resent the author? Why were they here if they didn't admire Mira Wallacz? People couldn't admit they admired anyone at all or that something they read gave them pleasure? Were people too hardened or

too vulnerable? Geneva Finch felt more innocent than these people and, at the same time, at twenty years old—older.

It's not like she couldn't be jealous herself. Still, it wasn't like
Mira Wallacz had hurt anyone, had she? Or maybe she had? Maybe
something in her writing made people feel wounded?

Really, Mira Wallacz should be an inspiration, indicating that
yes, a life can be lived in nearly any way a person wants—maybe—
as long as the person isn't a serial killer or any kind of killer, really.
So why not be grateful? And by now someone should announce if
Mira Wallacz had returned or was still missing. Possibly, the festival organizers, whoever they were, didn't want to acknowledge the
gossip about how their featured author had gone missing.

Maybe Geneva Finch wasn't entirely alone in feeling the way
she did. She couldn't be the only one at the conference who was
there out of love and respect. And gratitude. Mira Wallacz's novels had given Geneva's mother nearly miraculous moments that
muffled pain. Those novels let Geneva and her mother find themselves in the midst of imaginative adventures, casual, haphazard
adventures. The novels were romantic too, not in a gushy way, not
in a realistic way either, thank god. Life was better in Mira Wallacz's novels. Crimes were solved and love endured and enormous
cakes were baked and sliced and eaten. Oh the food—so delicious.
Desserts called "trifles" with heaps of whipped cream and candied
yellow roses. And lavender-infused concoctions and sliced ginger
arrayed around eggplant in white sauce and more cheeses than
Geneva imagined ever existed. And comforting things—like scal-
loped potatoes with heavy cream and a spattering of nutmeg. And
there were terraces overlooking vast bodies of water and people
who had all the time in the world to live inside the mysteries surrounding them. You could survive in that pleasurable glass globe
for a while and forget everything else. Well, someone always died in

the novels, that was true, but usually right at the start and it wasn't anyone you got to know, and in the end justice was accomplished by someone not entirely unlike whoever you imagined you might become.

What Geneva felt for Mira Wallacz—it was almost too much, almost like love. If she told anyone how she felt she would be dismissed and misunderstood. That movie with Kathy Bates, about being the author's biggest fan and then tying the poor author to the bed and cutting off his thumb and pushing it into his birthday cake—or was she mis-remembering? If she told anyone they would think she was one click away from being that awful character in *Misery*.

And now, if Mira Wallacz wasn't going to appear, there wasn't really a reason for Geneva Finch to stay at the conference. Maybe she should leave. But no—Mira Wallacz might turn up yet. At least Geneva was here to celebrate the author, to plant the flag of admiration. Even if she never met Mira Wallacz she should still think it was worth it, just to be on the grounds where the author spent time. She wasn't really an obsessive fan, after all. Not some stalker.

She settled on the couch in the lobby behind an artificial palm and opened the conference program. Inside: two photographs of Mira Wallacz. One must have been taken when the author was not too many years older than Geneva. Below, in a more recent photograph, the novelist stared into the camera, her eyes narrowed and her expression challenging. Geneva felt her spine stiffen. You need to learn to be like that, she thought: clear-eyed, focused, purposeful. She couldn't imagine Mira Wallacz ducking her head in fear of anyone.

On the fold-out: a list of speakers with photographs. She recognized two of the women from the lakeside. There was Tama Squires, her chin propped by her fist, identified as a biographer. The photograph made her look flirtatious. Photographs lie, but maybe this one revealed how the biographer wanted to be seen. Although probably Tama Squires didn't even need to flirt. She would say exactly what she wanted in any situation and be likely to get whatever she desired through sheer force of will. Flirting would be too slow and unproven a tactic. And yet—under that self-assurance maybe there was something gullible. A child-like quality in the eyes, not quite innocent but stubborn, the way children can be. If Geneva's instincts were right, Tama Squires was so sure of herself she could be fooled more easily than she ever suspected. That was the weak spot with imperious people: flattery.

Luisa Chaudette's photograph made her look stern and fussy, with a glare in her dark eyes and two vertical lines deepening above her nose. She was identified as a "prominent novelist." Maybe the photograph was a disguise too, like Tama Squires's. Luisa Chaudette wanted to be seen as serious, a person of high intelligence and great integrity. When she had listened to her by the lake Geneva had the impression that Luisa Chaudette didn't trust herself. The nice things she said about Mira Wallacz were delivered almost resentfully.

And there was Inger Delft, the publisher—whose second talk, after her session on the "art and craft of publishing," was called "The Future of Mira Wallacz." In the photograph she looked shiny, actually oiled. She was staring upward, as if inspiration was about to strike in her luminous world.

Geneva knew she was being judgmental and jumping to conclusions and trying to convince herself she could be profound. It was a habit. Her mother once said, "The way you try to get under the skin of people and what they're thinking—if you weren't my own daughter I'd be terrified of you." Saying that, her mother had laughed. Anyway, Geneva never meant to terrify anyone. She was always the one terrified. If she listened closely for what anyone said it was because she had needed to. She'd dealt with people who said one thing and hid something else—her mother's doctors, the insurance company, the agencies purportedly formed to help people like her and her mother. It's how people sound that gives them away. That, and their eyes.

When Geneva returned to her room the older woman's suitcase and hairnet were gone. Maybe her roommate had had enough of the place, given that people said Mira Wallacz left without warning and might not show up again. As for herself, Geneva was glad to have time in the room alone. Other people made friends easily, whereas she was either silent or wandering around lonely as a cloud—like in that awful poem. A year ago she wouldn't have made that connection about clouds. That was before she read the line of poetry in Mira Wallacz's latest novel.

Maybe Mira Wallacz wasn't even lost. Maybe she was in the conference building, wandering by herself. Or maybe she fell and twisted her ankle in a rabbit burrow in the woods by the lake. It seemed heartless, Geneva realized, to stay in her room when she should be searching for the author.

For the next half hour she made her way around the conference center looking for the author and then, feeling hopeless, sat through part of a video projection of the covers of Mira Wallacz's books for children juxtaposed with the covers of her novels. She listened to a woman argue that all those covers had something to do with one another. A really whack conspiracy theory. No one mentioned that Mira Wallacz was lost. Possibly that meant she was found and it would be embarrassing to go on and on about how people mistakenly thought—or hoped—she vanished.

Geneva lingered by a table of donuts left over from an early morning session. The donut she bit into was already hard. The coffee from the hot plate was still hot although burned. She walked down the hall until she found an empty room and sat in a padded chair, the seat under her wonderfully soft, and at once she was crying into her hands, shaking with an over-brimming sense of relief and something like joy, a sneaking joy. The sheer luck. She even had a room of her own at the conference. She was going to meet Mira Wallacz if there was any chance of meeting her at all—because of course the novelist would be back. Everything was going to be all right. And here Geneva was. She'd made it despite the two awful bus rides and the boy tossing the ball and hanging over the seat to intimidate her. She might as well be a character in one of Mira Wallacz's novels, one of the women who discovered who the murderer was and escaped being murdered herself.

"Why do you think she tried to be anonymous for all those years?" Luisa Chaudette was asking Yolanda, whose last name Luisa never caught. They were drinking a very red very forgettable wine on a burgundy-colored couch in a side room off the lobby. The couch was perfect—you didn't have to worry about anyone noticing where you spilled your wine. "What was the harm in people knowing her identity?"

Yolanda pushed at a couch pillow, drawing it to her lap. "I think she believed not being known would make her life easier. Maybe it was pretentiousness on her part, keeping a secret, you know? It couldn't last. Obviously she felt a need to crack out of her shell, and social media helped. You know how in her novels the victim always has some occupation no one ever heard of? Like professional onanist? I'm kidding, I'm kidding. It's like she was ashamed of her own occupation as a novelist. That it was too egotistical. Like, at first, she thought she could erase her identity. Maybe she didn't want the responsibility of being visible to her readers and now she's erasing herself again by taking off from the festival. It takes a lot of hubris to do that at a festival about your own work."

Luisa volunteered, "Or maybe this has all been exhausting. Everyone focusing on her. And now all this fretting. Crazy stuff. I heard at registration that she still hasn't shown up. She missed the last three panels yesterday and dinner and never turned up for a session today when she was supposed to be introducing the speaker."

Yolanda set her glass on the side table. "She's always been a tease—a difficult person to deal with. An airy sort of person. I used to talk to her about tree spirits. She'd scoff and then whatever I said turned up in her writing. She really does use me for her work—a little too much. Friendship like that can be hard."

"Why are you friends with her if—"

Yolanda twisted her hands before plucking up and kneading another pillow. "Why are we friends? I suppose we nettle each other in a productive way. For her it's productive, anyway. I see all the smoke and mirrors and she knows it." She tossed the pillow aside, picked up her glass, sipped, and set the glass down so hard it could have shattered.

Two younger women looked up from the next couch before turning away.

Yolanda continued. "Then again, maybe I should reconsider what friendship means to Mira. How can you be friends with someone, truly friends, when that person keeps half of their life secret—in fact, the most interesting part? Until her agent outs her. You know, Mira's face went slack when she looked out at the audience during that panel presentation yesterday morning. Eyes going sparkless. I can't remember much of what she talked about anyway. Her love of wallpaper, that's all I remember. How she created an archive of wallpaper patterns from each place in her life where something meaningful happened to her. Right there, I caught her in a lie. What are the chances that all those places had wallpaper? Who even uses wallpaper anymore? You catch someone in a lie like that and doubt pinballs back through everything they say. She didn't allow questions yesterday morning—that was a dead giveaway too. For years, with me, she used to sit there listening, shoveling everything I said into her mind until it came out replanted in her characters. I should get at least half of her royalties. My own mind is in those books, twisted into another shape, but it's there in the midst of all that garbage—"

"It's not exactly garbage."

"The style isn't refined. Whereas her children's books—those were where her heart was, her soul. The novels were—"

"Her genitals?" Luisa said, smiling.

"When she gifted me that first novel, she pretended she didn't write the thing, that she picked it up at an independent bookstore in Maine because the cover reminded her of me. If you remember the edition—it's the one with the wolf climbing a cherry tree? The cherries are immense, two on a stem, and the wolf is tiny and grey and toothless, with big droopy gums." Yolanda paused. She wished she had told someone her thoughts back then, wished she had said: I suspect Mira Wallacz is trying to seduce me with that novel—all those blasted sex scenes. *She leaves much to the imagination*—that's what about five hundred lunatics said on Goodreads. Mira leaves much to the imagination because she's probably never had sex. Or a spiritual experience that's better than sex.

"I have that edition," Luisa said. "Best cover ever."

Bonanza! Geneva Finch discovered a platter of sugar cookies at the back of a meeting room and slipped three on a paper plate and sat down to enjoy them. Another panel presentation. One woman with beautiful wild pink hair that rose in spirals was lecturing at a long table.

"I really wasn't sure if I should take her on," the woman said, her mouth hovering just above her microphone. "That first manuscript—the repetitive rhymes were sweet—but the drawings. I really thought we should use a professional artist. Then I was visiting my cousin and her child saw the drawings—I had the manuscript with me, tucked in my satchel—and her face lit up. Those drawings were unskilled. Surprisingly, though, they conveyed something to children. Mira knows a secret language, a visual language, that only children know and then forget as they grow up. Pitching that book was horrible, but I kept saying, 'Just try this out on a kid.'

"It looked like it had to be a one-off. But then those bunnies went on their adventures—inside their little homes. Every adventure between the dining room, the kitchen, and the 'parlor.' She loves that word, 'parlor.' So do kids. Secretly every child is a Victorian."

The audience laughed. The laughter didn't stop the woman from talking. "Before Mira, we were a small, unknown boutique agency. Most of what came over the transom: the dregs of dregs. Until we acquired Mira. Then we got the dregs of the dregs plus some really fabulous children's book authors: Gilcrint and Foster Bligh and Piper Fields and Avery Ogabe."

A question came from the audience—Geneva couldn't make it out.

The pink-haired woman again bent to her microphone: "I can't say I'm totally unfamiliar. I mentioned that I nearly finished two of her novels, right? We only dealt with her children's books. About the adult novels—I don't know what we would have done if those came to us as manuscripts. The murders were almost incidental. To the orgies."

A general peeling off by nearly everyone. A quieting. In an alcove in the next hallway Tama was holding forth to three women whose names she didn't bother to catch. "It wasn't exactly like Patricia Highsmith and Henry Miller mated to produce her. Given her nature images, there would need to be a third parent involved: possibly William Wordsworth."

Soon, even Tama was tired of talking. One of the women, taller than Tama and clasping a violent handbag that kept banging her side, accidentally nudged Tama with her elbow.

Which helped Tama decide that it might be a good time either to step outside or to return to her room or somehow or other face what was beginning to ripple throughout the conference: the expectation that Mira Wallacz might never come back. Really, someone should go looking for her. Seriously, not in a half-assed way. Besides, Lizette was late but she would, eventually, arrive. Without Mira, the conference was becoming claustrophobic, like everyone was gossiping about a ghost.

While lying flat on her hotel room bed, Luisa Chaudette mentally tortured herself.

I had never been entirely sure it was Mira in the water, Luisa reminded herself, and then, after all, it wasn't Mira. I have nothing to confess, nothing to be sorry for. And Mira taking off, vanishing even though she was supposed to be on panels or at least in

attendance, etcetera. And now making everyone suspicious. Forc-
ing people to search for her. Plus, as for drowning, Mira Wallacz
was the one who put the idea into Luisa's head with her novels—
two of which involved complicated drownings. It's hard to create
a world out of your own imagination, and then someone like Mira
comes along and it's so easy for her that it's positively exhibition-
istic. A recollection, sludgy around the edges, arrived for Luisa. At
another festival seven years ago: everyone was listening to a young
poet recite from his new book. On one side of the room a giant window filled an entire wall. And while the young poet read his earnest
poems, outside that window in full view of everyone in the room
strode a famous poet wearing tiny electric blue swimming briefs.
The famous poet mounted the ladder to the diving board. Even the
poet at the podium turned to the window. The entire room gawked,
engrossed in watching the renowned poet preparing to dive. And
the lesser-known poet picked up the papers from which he had
been reading his poems, walked away from the podium, and ex-
ited the room, while everyone else continued to gape at the famous
poet, now executing laps. Jesus Christ, some people deserve to die.

▸▸ Chapter Four

MIRA WALLACZ WAS THINKING about a children's book she never sold. Failures, how they never let you go. The plot was simple, naturally. The bunnies perch fluffily on a window ledge—very catlike, those bunnies—observing the rain. One bunny says to the other, "Wow, this rain sure is coming fast!" And the other bunny says, "Everything's going to be soggy, Oggy." Outside the window a duck floats in a mud puddle. Oggy says, "Everything's soggy except that duck." "Yeah," the other bunny says, "We could do that too! We should swin around in that puddle." And then the bunny who's not Oggy goes on to say, "Let's do it, Oggy!" The bunnies press themselves against the window glass, which is smudged with their fur. Then the bunnies look out from the page into the eyes of the child reading the book, and Oggy says, "We did it!" Even though they're still inside the house, the bunnies make swimming gestures with their fluffy paws. On the last pages the duck and the bunnies are together, swimming past the sofa, past the armchair, past the coffee table, past every window. A book for children who are shut in, who can't get out of their own houses.

The heat was unusual for October and for so late in the afternoon. It must be after three. No doubt Mira Wallacz would have been better off taking a taxi or an Uber back to the conference hotel where she could strip off the wet skin of her blouse and turn the air conditioner on high. That would make sense, but since when had sense ever served her? Plus, she had something she had to do.

Minutes ago she was walking beside the road when she heard a car in the distance. She stepped into the ditch and headed up a small wooded hill to avoid being seen. Hadn't that always been her problem—being seen? People thinking they knew her, ascribing motives to her, bad intentions. That's what being seen can amount to, if you're not careful. And now she was ready not to be seen again, possibly to fade away, or to write under another pseudonym, maybe in a different genre if she could manage the challenge. Or maybe not write at all. Quit. That would actually be an adventure. Stopping.

She moved into less heated pockets of air, the sweat from her walk cooling her neck. A frustrating day. She wondered if the message she'd left was ever received. Everyone should have a cell phone. People who didn't—they were from another world. Amazing they could still function. A wind gust sent leaves thrashing high above her.

The conference center had to be up ahead, past where the lake rounded. What an absurd idea to host a festival, a conference, or whatever Stephanie called it—and already Mira's experience was proving once again how wonderful it would be to assume anonymity. She'd agreed to the festival because of these woods and because she grew up not far from here, where her mother had lived.

She was passing into the leaning shadow under the limbs of an oak when she endured a wash of unreality. Just ahead: a pond, oily-looking, the water swirling like a scald. Under her feet the dry leaves spewed dust. So many leaves. Old autumns crusted upon other autumns. She looked up at the maple crowned with yellow leaves, the lower branches already balding. She lowered her gaze toward the horizon.

That was when she saw the girl between the trees.

Geneva Finch was shaking as she ran to Mira. "You left us!" she shouted.

"What are you talking about?"

"We all came for you. I came just to see you. I took a bus! Two buses!"

Mira stepped back. "You're seeing me now, aren't you?"

Geneva Finch and Mira Wallacz stared at one another. Geneva told herself: Remember. Remember this. To see Mira Wallacz, to find her here in the woods, among the trees. To be alone with her. Everything in Geneva's range of sight was whitening out, as in a blizzard, except the snow was all inside her eyes. Gradually Mira Wallacz's face appeared before her again—a wide-eyed face, her mouth half smiling (like in photos online!). Then the skin shivered on Mira Wallacz's jaw. It was like a closeup on a movie screen, like Geneva's sight could magnify anything. The author's eyes were greenish with gold sprinkles. Eye freckles.

I'm standing too close, Geneva realized. She lowered her gaze out of courtesy and saw that Mira Wallacz was wearing tennis shoes, the kind colored like old ivory tusks. Geneva looked up again. Wide black straps on Mira Wallacz's shoulders. A backpack. Mira Wallacz was backpacking. Was that what all the fuss was about? Mira Wallacz disappeared from the festival to go backpacking.

A shift in the air, a sudden chill, the temperature plummeting. The prickling on Geneva's scalp, buzzing in her ears. Overcome by instinct in one of the most urgent moments of her life, Geneva Finch took Mira Wallacz's hand, pulling her. Mira should be horrified by this stranger propelling her forward, Mira's hand clasped by this truly weird girl and the trees rushing by as they ran and ran, and there, a ways ahead, the lake, gray and dim and the air whizzing next to Mira's ears. The two of them were holding hands as in a game for children, and in that unexpected moment Mira was transported into her past and once again felt what it was to be a lonely little girl whose mother couldn't love her.

But no, she was a middle aged woman, her legs flying out from under the rest of her.

Strange, strange, strange. But beautiful—to be almost flying, and then as they both slowed—Mira felt the girl's terror. Electric sparks. They stumble-ran and stopped to get their breath. The skin of Mira's face was shrinking. The air, full of slapping hands. And then they were hurtling forward again, dead leaves scattering. They kept running until they felt the shore's pebbles under their feet and Mira bent, hands on her knees. At last when she regained her breath she looked at the girl and asked, "What are we running from? You can tell me. Why did you want us to run?"

The girl was still gasping. Her crooked teeth—the teeth of poverty. The smell of mold coming from her—her clothes had to be dirty. A certain sickliness in the girl's face, the dimness of her eyes. Mira wondered if girls like this one found themselves in her novels—the buried seed, the pain and exhaustion and hopelessness of hunger. Eating only toast with jam and the toast moldy. The mold in the house not just on the bread. The burst pipes, the old walls cracked to the ceiling. But maybe, even so, the girl staring at Mira had been loved for years. Don't remember your own childhood, Mira. That's not your problem anymore.

This girl could vanish off the face of the earth so easily. Girls like this one too often did. Mira couldn't know if she'd done any good for anyone like this girl. Maybe she'd harmed all of those girls who read her novels, led them astray, allowed them to think that uncovering any mystery could be done without consequences to themselves.

"Why did you want us to run?" Mira repeated. She didn't expect the girl to answer. Probably the girl had no idea why.

Geneva kept her voice low. "There was something wrong—someone was watching."

Mira looked off through the treeline toward the direction of the conference center beyond the lake's rim.

"We should get back," Geneva said, her voice shaking. "Everyone's worried. They were going to call the police, I think. They said you wandered off. People do that—wandering off. My mother—she—"

Mira flinched. "Listen, honey. I need some time out here to clear my mind. And I need to do a little something, and for that I need time. Here in the woods. Anyway, I'm not quite ready to go back. You know what that's like? You feel like people want too much from you? I don't mean that you want too much. You seem like a nice girl. No need to tell anyone you found me here. That would make me seem pathetic, you know?"

"I know."

"You go back and we'll talk later."

Mira didn't plan to explain her absence to anyone, how she had taken the bus into Pewter yesterday afternoon. Wanted to see the retreat lodge that was for sale, then stayed overnight at a motel. Didn't imagine she could be missed all that much at the conference center. Had called to leave a message with a friend. Waited at a lunch place, waited for too long. Until it was clear her message must have been misunderstood. On the way back to the conference center she made the bus driver drop her off on the side of the road because she had to visit the path her mother used to walk. *Whose woods these are I think I know.* The words came so easily in memory.

Her mother had recited them often to Mira and their next door neighbor.

The girl was backing away. One of those transparent girls, traumatized, expectant. All soulful yearning. Maybe every book Mira wrote was never harmful and was really meant for those girls locked inside the women they became? Gestated like a twin. No, that was unkind. A girl could always peep out and then be soothed and taught—if someone cared enough—to put on her armor, to refuse to harbor the oldest pain, the loss of a mother's love or, worse, never to have known that sort of love.

Mira waited until Geneva Finch was a gray shadow disappearing between trees. Waited more. Then turned and headed back to the path in the woods. The girl's strange scramble—taking Mira's hand—hurtling with her down the slope, breathless, panting—had interrupted Mira's attempt to find the place between two small hills where a stream caught light and flowed down to the lake, a stream that clarified the leaves caught there, turning them golden. A place she'd been told about. She'd never before had the courage to search the place out, to step where she was never wanted until it was too late.

The leaves underfoot were dry and crackled and released the sounds of the stirrings of birds or squirrels, and then—just as must have happened to Geneva—Mira endured a quickening sensation. Her scalp tensed, her body knowing before her mind. She turned around and around. And whatever it was—something fallen from a tree and hurled by a wind gust?—whatever it was passed beside her forehead, careening so close the air snapped.

Three women in the restaurant shouted. For there Mira Wallacz was, fully visible through the giant window, heading out from the trees. Mira, playing innocent. Or–no. It wasn't Mira. It was a young girl, looking either ecstatic or gut-shot.

Unlike the conference attendees at the window, Geneva Finch, heading into the lobby, believed she knew what would happen next. Mira Wallacz would turn up soon, maybe a half hour later. She would then be surrounded by well-wishers in the lounge, and she would keep nodding her head and smiling. Mira Wallacz, acting baffled by questions. So sorry to confuse anyone, Mira would keep saying, and have you met Geneva, my marvelous new friend? And how good it would be for Geneva to tell her mother—although there was no telling her mother anything now. Hah—a fantasy. Mira Wallacz would not even remember her. Still, Mira Wallacz had talked with her, hadn't brushed her hand away. If only Geneva's mother were still alive. If only Geneva could make up for everything that was lost to her mother.

What Geneva could not escape: she had not been a good daughter. When her mother was alive Geneva used to run out of the house to escape her own feelings of rage. Not rage at her mother, rage at their situation, and yet one part of her could hardly disconnect rage from what she saw of her mother's suffering. And then later she feared she had hastened her mother's death, that her mother felt herself to be a terrible burden, had wanted to die.

"And God will help us, just give him your hand," Geneva's mother had advised her daughter. Geneva should have changed the sheets more often, should have made healthier meals, should have found a way to get a job that paid better, should have filled out more forms when her mother was denied the help she needed. Should have. Geneva endured days when she pulled herself out of bed each morning by imagining herself being drawn upright by a giant hand. She told her mother about it, confessed really. "That's God's hand," her mother said.

It would have given her mother such happiness to know that her own daughter met Mira Wallacz and touched her.

Tama Squires, back in her hotel room, got to work composing an email:

Tallyho—

Located an old friend of Mira's: Yolanda Eng or Something-or-Other. My suspicion: she's got an appetite for dishing the dirt and digging up the grub.

Mira Wallacz has left the festival or anyway she's nowhere to be found. Here's just hoping Mira disappears a couple more times for the dramatic value. You should see the interest Mira is stirring. In a fit of projection, people actually imagined she drowned in the lake. I played with that idea too—tantalizing. Or else they think she'll hop out of the forest, like one of her rabbits, except her agoraphobic rabbits never leave their crappy cottages.

Additional wine and cheese are about to be had in the third-floor conference room and this woman I met—Luisa Chaudette, she writes absolute crap—is scheduled to give a tribute to Mira—once Mira returns. Also, some Swede hinted about a rebuttal. Must attend, I suppose. If only to watch the back of Mira Wallacz's head! Once again, as you can imagine, it's all research. And research, research, research doesn't come cheap! I have such a good feeling—people are going to be interested in Mira Wallacz more than ever—very soon. Trust my instincts on this.

PART TWO

⯈ CHAPTER FIVE

ECAUSE SHE was one of the last persons to see Mira Wallacz alive—perhaps the very last, it was suspected—Geneva Finch sat on the bottom bunk in her room at the convention center hotel answering questions.

If you try to look innocent you look guilty. It's like trying not to appear insane. That's obvious. Everyone says that. And she couldn't stop her hands from jumping. Of course the police only wanted to secure as much information as they could—about Mira Wallacz's state of mind, they claimed.

"She seemed fine. She was kind to me. She must have been backpacking. She had a backpack. She said she had something she needed to do in the woods. She wanted me to leave."

The smirk from the policewoman: "And did that make you angry, that she wanted you to leave her alone?"

And Geneva's muddy answer. "I admired her. I came just to see her—at the festival. I didn't care about the other authors—only her."

The officer: "You're her biggest fan?"

"I've read all Mira Wallacz's novels. I wouldn't hurt her."

The other officer: "Did anyone say you should hurt her?"

The police officers suspected her, didn't they? Weren't they right to suspect her? She would suspect herself!

A local boy tromping through the woods had found the body with rocks around it and didn't disturb the scene. He was cleared instantly—locals spoke for him, even the Catholic priest vouched for him. The boy worked for the diocese. Most likely Mira Wallacz died in a freak accident. Falling rocks. A simple explanation exists for most things. That made sense, didn't it?

Probably plenty of people at the festival were questioned. But Geneva came forward first and admitted she saw Mira Wallacz after everyone else said she vanished. Which meant, she kept reminding herself, she was the last, other than the murderer—if there was a murderer and it wasn't a freak accident.

How many times did Geneva Finch try to convince herself that Mira Wallacz's death was an accident?

Every day.

Every day for ten years.

And during those years Geneva thought about how she was instructed by Mira Wallacz not to tell anyone she had seen her. What Geneva told the police was true: Mira Wallacz had been kind and Geneva had obeyed her.

She didn't say she believed Mira almost knew her, really saw her, that even her past was seen. Maybe not in terms of the particulars. Mira must have imagined what a certain sort of life does to you when you have no help to speak of and you attend a mother's long illness and the place you lived—"you're lucky to have a roof over your head"—was peeling away—peeling wallpaper with rot in the ceiling and plaster in piles and the dark mold in the walls and how at school the other girls won't look at you because of that problem with your back, the problem you corrected by lying on the floor, stretching, putting lifts in your shoes from the school nurse—and after school always going home to the smell of the house, the smell that wouldn't leave, and how you learned to walk a certain way to look a little less funny even while you made yourself smaller, so small not to be worth noticing. And then after high school you went to community college and a new life began and at that festival ten years ago you actually met Mira Wallacz, who looked at you with sympathy. As if she knew. And, once again, the mold—it was ridiculous to think that Mira knew about that. These are things you can't tell anyone. Can't even explain.

How lucky she felt to come upon Mira Wallacz there in the woods—but soon after Geneva left her, Mira died. Geneva could not understand it, how Mira could have died, how rocks from the cliffside had leapt out of place and attacked her.

A half-memory. Her mother lifting a sea shell, its pink the inside of a rabbit's ear—and setting the shell back on the shelf in the tourist shop. And watching in horror when the shell rolled and fell and struck a glass cabinet and then, with what seemed like demonic force, struck Geneva. The top of five-year-old Geneva's head spurted—a blood patty. That was how the store clerk described it. And then the frantic drive to Emergency, and the nurses claimed Geneva's mother was in shock and tried to bar her from entering the room where Geneva would be examined. "I won't leave her"— her mother's stern voice rang out. Next: new pressure on the top of Geneva's skull and a row of stitches and finally two nurses giggled when her mother explained what happened and said "conch shell."

One thing Geneva Finch knew even as a small child. There's so much blood with a head wound. Mira Wallacz must have suffered.

The knock on the roof of her car startled Geneva.

Aida was shouting, her hair purple under the streetlight, her mouth close to smushed against the car's window. "Don't make me face those assholes alone. Come on, Finchster. Let's do this."

Geneva let her window down. "I wasn't invited."

"I hardly know these people and I was invited. Come on, Finchie, I'm sure it's an oversight."

Aida had been hired four months ago. She was direct and funny and bossy and irreverent—in other words likely to get into trouble. She was already being treated by their boss Elson with sniffy contempt.

"Listen," Aida said. "Obviously they meant to invite you. You've been working with Elson longer than they have. You're indispensable—even for this idiotic party."

All week long Geneva heard about the party at work, and so when she drove to CVS to pick up a few things she swung by the block and parked across from the party house. Just curiosity. And now here was Aida, outing her.

"You go on in," Geneva said. "You mind not telling anyone about my—"

"Your being out here hunched in your car like a creep? You were lurking. Come on, Geneva. Let's make this party more interesting. Besides, you need to cheer me up. Did you know that Elson is probably going to fire me? Apparently I'm aggressive and rude to clients."

Geneva got out of the car. "Oh no—he can't do that! He knows you're aggressive and rude. He knew that when he hired you. He won't fire you. I'll talk to him."

The rings on Aida's fingers flashed under the streetlight. "Don't, Geneva. Don't. He'll fire you first. Come on. Make me happy in my agony. Let's go inside."

"What if Elson's in there?"

"He definitely wasn't invited." She waved a beer bottle in front of Geneva's face. On the label, a tiny man wielding an ax.

Geneva was thinking that in many relationships one person gets to be Lucy and the other gets to be Ethel. Geneva didn't think she'd ever be Lucy and she didn't want to be Ethel either. Nevertheless, on occasions like this it was hard not to fall into position.

A few steps into the party house's foyer and Geneva already felt newly unsettled. The fug of weed, a rotten hay smell. Nearly every inch of the walls blistered with a movie poster or a devil mask. She hoped to recognize someone despite the dim light. Maybe these guests were just personal friends of Clement and Suze's.

The coffee table—at least that was familiar—was pushed into the corner of the room. Two women in head wraps were rolling up a strip of carpet. Three giddy women in short, lacy, nearly identical dresses danced together, waving their arms in the air. Interestingly worm-like motions. Professional dancers? That made sense: Clement and Suze handled accounts for so-called "exotic" acts.

When would the hosts appear and realize Geneva crashed their party?

She blinked, her eyes aching from the smoke. When she opened her eyes again a face—almost a familiar face—was very close, like a balloon blown up before her eyes.

She knew this man. Not enough to say he wasn't a stranger, and yet she knew his face.

Seconds later she understood. His face was stationed above the ad for The Tompkins Givens Guitar Duo, for whom she'd booked a show. She had checked the local free newspaper to make sure the ad appeared. She considered the man's photograph for a beat or two, that was all. She had read the headline, not the article that accompanied the photograph.

"You're okay?" the man asked, reaching out to her. "It looked like you were falling backward. You're all right?"

A ripple of fear shot up her arm where his hand rested. Degloved: the skin separated from muscle. Degloved was the term she learned when a neighbor's dog attacked a wild rabbit. Geneva and her mother—her once healthy, living mother—had taken the injured rabbit to the wildlife rehab center.

The man let go of her arm just as Aida hurried up. "She looked like she was ready to faint," he told Aida, sounding guilty.

"Oh, she does that," Aida said.

A generous smile, running up and into his eyes.

"I heard about you in the kitchen," Aida said. "You're an actual poet. You know what I say to that? Hope is not the thing with feathers."

The poet recited in a calm, clear voice: "Hope is the thing with feathers that perches in the soul and sings the tune without the words and never stops at all."

"Show off," Aida said. "Hobgoblin? I've got some more where this came from."

The poet nodded and Aida rushed out of the room.

"I've never liked that poem," the man told Geneva. "That bird has flown for me too many times."

"Well, there you go," Geneva said, feeling stupid. What did she know about poetry? Before she left college she researched Marianne Moore for an English course—and couldn't stop thinking about the poet's tricorn hat, a hat fit for a general. Nothing humble about that hat. Marianne Moore had to be an exhibitionist of the higher sort. Geneva didn't get a good grade on the paper.

Aida returned. "We're dancing now," she announced, setting down three beers on the coffee table. "Come on, Mr. Poet."

Just about everyone was dancing, tight against one another. After a while Geneva kept laughing as she danced and the floor began bouncing. Soon, all around her, it became the kind of dancing where people fall slowly and laugh on the floor. Geneva thought of videos where dancing people cause a floor to collapse and some of the people die. That other time when she was at Suze and Clement's house she hadn't realized how old and rickety the floor was. It was almost as if she was inside an entirely different house.

The obvious occurred to her: this was an entirely different house. Same block, different house.

The hosts didn't appear or, at any rate, she couldn't determine who they were among the guests. How unreal everything began to seem, like a stage set, the light smoky and the music unrecognizable and never stopping. The poet's face came close to hers and blotted out everything else, and then the poet pulled back and he looked like he was sipping something and his features ran together. By then, Geneva was sweaty, eel-like and slippery, and what did it matter.

She felt drunk but wasn't, not much, didn't need to be—although a half hour later she slid to the floor twice, and she loved how silly she felt. She was already trying to find words for the sensations she was experiencing. It was like nostalgia for the present moment. It was like, what else? Like the way she felt when rolling down a grassy hill as an eight-year-old.

After three in the morning Geneva drove the poet back to his hotel.

"I heard they serve great eggs there," she said. "Every morning's like Easter. I don't know what I'm talking about. That was kind of a while ago—Easter. Time has always been a problem for me. The

eggs aren't all hard-boiled at the hotel. It's not really like Easter."
Maybe she wasn't as sober as she thought.

"You celebrate Easter each year?" he asked. "Is that right? What did your family do for Easter?"

"We didn't really celebrate it much," Geneva said. "Well, my mother and I used to. I loved Easter back then. The bunny. The eggs. The hiding of the eggs. The baskets. The part about new life, rising out of the egg."

"Rising out of the egg? "

"You're not judging me, are you? I hate to be judged."

"You feel judged?"

"Not always."

"Your friend called you Finchette? Or is it Finchster? You're Teresa, but what's your last name?"

"It's Geneva Finch. My middle name is Teresa so you weren't entirely wrong. I'm Geneva Teresa Finch."

"Teresa fits you best. Thérèse—the Little Flower—the saint."

"I don't think I want to be referred to as a little flower. Or a saint."

"Saint Thérèse. She was brilliant and the stories about her . . . how after her death roses fell from the sky."

"That sounds nice—and also very daft. I'd like that—not to die, but to have flowers falling all around me."

"I already understand that about you."

It was a perfect night to be driving, no traffic. She rolled the driver-side window down to let in gusts of air.

He told her about a problem with the hotel where his hosts at the university set him up: he could hear what was happening in the room next to his. He didn't know if he'd ever get to sleep.

Did he want her to take him to her apartment? For the quiet, presumably?

"Poor you," she said. "I keep forgetting your name. You told me it, didn't you?"

She dropped him off at his hotel, drove back to her apartment, drank glass after glass of water, fell into bed. When she woke the next morning her heart ached—actually ached so much it felt like she strained a muscle in her chest. I'll never have a night like that again, she told herself. It was like being in love without the responsibility. To fall and keep falling and never harm yourself. Although that wasn't entirely true. Her hips, her upper thigh on her right side: the bruises from falling while dancing, those actually did ache.

Some nights you consign to memory. If you examined those nights or tried to repeat them you'd blow right through what you want to believe was enchanting. It would be worse than disappointing. The original memory would curl and shrink. You'd be left embarrassed by yourself. Or not. She had absorbed enough embarrassment in her life—enough that she felt there might not be room for much more. Besides, embarrassment was a small emotion. Just the same, her heart kept skidding around in her chest.

She couldn't find a copy of the community paper that printed the article about the poet's visit to the university. She didn't have the poet's number, could only half-remember his name and wasn't entirely sure she even remembered that much correctly. Which, at first, inhibited her online searches until she tried another spelling of his name: Thom Crystl. He had no Facebook, no Instagram, no website. So different from the agency's clients, with their websites and YouTube videos of their tours.

And then: a few hits. He had been giving readings on the East Coast most recently and would be participating in a workshop on the New Jersey shore in two weeks. A conference sort of thing with panels and workshops and probably fun oceanside parties.

She kept searching the next day on her work computer. More hits. An astounding fact came out in the third interview she skimmed: Thom Crystl used to be a priest. The interviewer somehow knew that information, although it wasn't volunteered by Thom Crystl in the piece. Another interesting fact: Thom Crystl changed his name after he left the priesthood. The article didn't mention what his original name was. One interview referred to his hometown, Bingle.

As a priest, had he been transferred at any time to the town where he was born? Geneva searched a parish catalogue from Bingle and a newsletter. And then—it took less than a half hour—she found what she was looking for. A fuzzy photograph. Recognizable, barely. There he was—the poet—standing with a group of parishioners at an orchard, holding a shovel and smiling. Father Kleist.

She sprang up, walked around her desk, paced in front of the bank of windows, could hardly contain herself. Father Kleist. Four years ago a writer revisited "the mysterious death of an acclaimed author" and tried to interview Geneva for what he called her "role" in that "harrowing episode." She blocked the journalists' calls. Nevertheless, she made sure to read his article when it appeared online. And printed a copy. And saw not only her own name—she was briefly mentioned—but also the name of the priest who inherited every one of Mira Wallacz's assets and had been a "person of interest": Father Thomas Kleist.

The sound of a repressed sneeze made her look up. Charlie Clements. Geneva was glad to see him—the real world, the safe world that he represented. He shifted on the creaking green leather couch. The buttons always bothered him and he let her know as much before he tossed down his magazine. "Nothing in this rag. You're the reader. Here you go." He handed over *The At-lantic.* An established habit. He often gave Geneva his magazines, liked to prove he was a cultured man who subscribed. Also liked to give her his wife's castoffs. His wife was another agency client and made a formidable Dolly Parton. He repeated his usual pitch. "Jacinth's always ordering online, and you can never tell what size the shoes really are. Well, they're cheap as hell. I hope you don't mind us off-loading them on you."

"No, I love them. They're so—whimsical. Can I pay you?"

"No need."

She slipped the magazine in her satchel to keep it from getting lost among the papers on her desk. She stashed the shoes with others from Jacinth in a box she kept under her desk. Some of the skirts she'd accumulated from Jacinth—too short by a mile—would go to Goodwill, but the shoes—if they fit Geneva only donated those with the most outrageous heels. In her fantasy life Geneva thought she might wear some of those heels. Also the glitter blouse, low-cut, impossible, and beautiful. It had to have been too snug for Jacinth.

Charlie crossed his ankles and said in his Sinatra voice, "You look bug-eyed, like you just saw a ghost. I'm going to make sure Elson gives you a raise. He must not be treating you right. When does the evil son of a bitch get back?"

"He should be in soon. Everything okay?"

"Just reconsidering the crap I'll put up with next month at Gadfly."

"Can I help?"

"Not yet. I have some ideas I want to spin by Elson. He needs to see me every once in a while to realize I've still got a few tricks." He winked, and for a flashing moment she saw his resemblance to Sinatra, his face skinnier than the older Sinatra's, all skeins and tangles. Because Sinatra had such a long career Charlie didn't have to worry too much about aging out. Unlike Caesar Corhant, who at fifty was a red-faced Elvis, his hair sprayed black, his voice quivery, his opportunities shrinking. Caesar, who even took Holy Communion dressed as Elvis. Caesar, sighted in the grocery store pushing a cart while wearing his white rhinestone-lined cape. Whereas Charlie hardly had to work to resemble Sinatra. Even without the pork pie hat, the jacket slung over his shoulder. Next month he was scheduled for a tribute to Sinatra at Gadfly, and Geneva was sure he was in the office to see about getting his contract renegotiated.

He was staring at her again, wiggling his eyebrows, trying to make her laugh. By every indication he should be the most annoying client. Wouldn't tolerate email. Always insisted on calling and more often on arriving to lodge his demands. Enjoyed throwing around what little weight he had. Yet Geneva liked him more than most clients—liked that he brought her his old magazines and his wife's cast off shoes and costumes and insisted on bringing his troubles to Elson—not, she thought, out of the worry that she couldn't handle whatever problem he created. He wanted to spare her effort, although he probably realized she would be the one Elson relied on to sort things out.

"Where's your sidekick?" Charlie asked.

"Aida? She's still at lunch."

"She's got the right idea. That girl always has the right idea. She just has a crude way of letting you know it. You know why I never give her my magazines? She doesn't have the maturity to read them with enough comprehension. You, however, you're thirsty for knowledge."

She was thirsty for knowledge, that was true. And because of her own efforts, she knew some things. No longer was she the girl she used to be—it took time and every self-help book she could afford to pick up, including some that weren't second-hand. No longer too insecure, too fearful, too withdrawn—too alert and yet too ready to play dead. No longer too lonely. So lonely for years she had felt like her ribs were spreading apart.

It took friends too. A friend, long gone now—overdose—three friends gone the same way—the friend gave her advice: "You can't walk like that. You're inviting someone to hurt you. Pull yourself up. Look like you've got somewhere to go to—fast. If you can't do it for yourself do it for me. Defend yourself. I need to see a girl who doesn't take shit."

Geneva considered seriously every bit of advice she received. Because for a while there was no one she trusted after her mother's death and after Mira Wallacz's. Although she had Mira's books to reread and could at least trust the voices in those books. Except for the last, posthumously published, the book that the reviews said predicted Mira Wallacz's death. Reading that one would be too painful. Geneva looked away those months when copies were stacked on the first table near the entrance at bookstores. Otherwise, she had all of Mira Wallacz's novels, first editions, read and re-read.

She saved them as well as a few things from the house where she had lived with her mother: the transparent glass statue of a goose—like warm ice on her dresser, and the shiny metal drinking glasses in neon colors, and the jar of cloth roses her mother made, and the clay rabbit figurine. Otherwise, there was so much she couldn't keep from her mother's house—the smell turned her stomach, the smell clung to things. A house has its own way of dying.

Months after her mother's death she gathered her strength and made her own way. First, she found an apartment although it had exposed pipes (will you be electrocuted while you shower?) and a vine that grew from a patch of soil in the north corner. And she managed to get along with the rowdy boy roommates but not the unforgettable girl who came to visit the roommates and humiliated her because Geneva's straw hat was silly-looking and because she made a bad choice with one of those boys.

Next, she rented the upstairs apartment in a brownstone. The landlord: she could hear him talk to his dog. Say good night to his dog. Say good morning to his dog. She began to love him when she heard him conduct longer conversations with his dog. He liked to lie beside his dog and smell the dog's paws. Geneva wanted this habit to be endearing. It might have been, if he had loved her.

Then her life turned lucky: she got another apartment and Elson hired her and said it was a good thing she wouldn't have much to unlearn. And Elson suspected she wasn't likely to be awed by clients, the performers and speakers and writers whose contracts she learned to draw up. They needed what Elson called "a firm hand." She probably wouldn't even know who they were—at first. Anyway, the clients weren't generally all that well known. Some worked the college circuit, even for small student organizations. Their travel itineraries, their "requirements," their schedules, their contracts—she'd get good at figuring out what was best for them.

If you're a '70s tribute band, Elson said, maybe you should accept 1970's profits. Geneva didn't agree, but she understood the problem. What those performers accomplished was an art, but not everyone wanted to be entertained by nostalgia. It was sad for some performers, and they grew resentful, their borrowed identities obliterated by time. She had first-hand experience after disastrously dating George Harrison from one of The Beatles tribute bands. Whenever there was a mirror behind her in a restaurant he was looking over her shoulder. Like he was staring at a mean ghost. She was relieved when he hit on Aida. It gave Geneva an opportunity to offload the relationship without wounding him and turning him into a danger to herself. She might have been wounded herself by the relationship but by then she was exhausted. Practicing admiration takes too much out of a person. She still negotiated contracts for his group but wondered how long they'd command an audience. Given their ages they might do better if regrouping as The Rolling Stones.

Aida hustled into the office. Elson was right behind her, his yellow shirt faded and too tight. Disconcertingly, he looked like a member of one of the '70s tribute bands the agency represented.

"Just the fellow I want to see," Charlie shouted.

"Jesus," Elson moaned.

"No," Charlie said, "just me, you lousy bastard."

When they disappeared into Elson's office, Geneva asked Aida to meet her for break.

"I need your advice. It's about something I learned about that poet. The one at the party?"

"Oh great," Aida said. "Nothing makes me happier than giving advice. Let me ruin your life! That's not something you can do all by yourself!"

⊁ Chapter Six

G ENEVA AND AIDA chose the bench farthest from the building and its immense black windows. An airless day, the sun heating the top of Geneva's head. She found an old hairband in her purse and pulled her hair into a bun.

Aida opened a cup of yogurt and unwrapped a sandwich she'd rejected from lunch, pulled out the lettuce and placed it on the plastic wrap. "That party? You've been thinking about that party?" she said. "It must have been a better party for you than for me. Terrible dancing. And the poet—I remember him because he looked so clean. Like a dentist. Like he scrubbed his face. Very shiny." She wiped yogurt from her nose. "Ugggh. My spoon keeps slipping."

Geneva hesitated before she said, "You won't believe this. That poet we met—he used to be a priest."

"No."

"He's lapsed, or what do you call it—"

"He did something awful? Plenty of them do."

"I don't know about that. He left and changed his name."

"I don't think priests change their names. Nuns do. The patriarchy..."

"He decided to change his. I read it in an interview. You know what else? Remember my telling you about Mira Wallacz—the writer who died? She left everything to him."

Aida put down her yogurt and brushed off her skirt before she said, "No wonder he quit the church. He's rich. Lucky you. Obviously he liked you. You should find where he lives and surrender yourself. That's not unattractive. Surrendering."

"He gave the money away. To his parish."

"That's hard to believe. I mean, people say things like that, but there's always money in reserve they're hiding. How do you know all this? You paid off a detective?"

"I've been doing some pretty heavy searching online. The name of the priest was in an article when Mira's death was written about again—a few years ago. He must have been a suspect because he stood to gain from Mira's death. He was serving Mass at the time of her death. He was completely cleared."

"I don't understand how he turned up at that party—"

"It's only a coincidence."

Aida picked at her sandwich. "And now he's a poet and you say he has no money—I doubt that—but if it's true he lives on what? Or does poetry pay?"

"He teaches workshops. He's at festivals."

Aida made a sound between a snort and a chuckle. "I think it was all planned—somehow. This guy who couldn't stand being a priest for the rest of his life was at that party because of you. He wanted to get to know you—to see if you killed that writer? Your name—was it in that article about Mira's death? Could he have searched your name?"

"It was just a quick mention, and the article didn't exactly go viral. It's not even online anymore."

"I thought the internet was forever."

"The piece was posted in a literary journal. They're not forever."

Aida finished the last of her sandwich before she said, "Anyway, he might have found out who you are. Maybe he suspects you killed her? It's too much of a coincidence, his being there at that party—even though we were at the wrong house and everything that happened that night was entirely random. He has to know who you are. Maybe he's got a friend in the police force—priests have friends in odd places. They know where all the bodies are buried. They're notorious for that, police and priests. He knew more about the investigation than you did, I'm betting. He was searching for you, and then when he saw you're such a bad, sloppy dancer and such an innocent he decided you didn't have enough stamina to kill anyone. You kept saying meeting him was a coincidence. Whatever it was, what are you going to do about it?"

"What do you mean?"

"You're not going to contact him or try to find out more about what happened to—what's her name, the writer who either was or was not murdered? She was stoned to death?"

"Hearing it described like that—Aida, I left her alone in the woods. I went back to the conference center, just like she asked and I left her. I was terrified when I was in the woods with her. It was sudden—this awful feeling. I took her hand and ran with her. I felt like the threat was somehow above us."

"Like—flying witches? Or like—in the trees?"

"I don't know. I shouldn't have left her alone."

"What? You did what she asked, right? She asked you to leave? You always do what you're asked. That's one of your faults. I mean, I like it when you do what I ask, but you have to be careful about who's doing the asking."

Geneva smiled and said, "Aida, could you be any more condescending?"

"Yes. Of course. I'm sorry, Geneva. Let me tell you a story. It will be interesting."

"Oh, please, no."

They stared at one another. Aida began, "When I was a kid a salesman came to our house. I could see him from my bedroom window getting out of his car. In our front room my brother was playing a clarinet—making it shriek—I mean, really shriek, like a screaming woman. When the salesman got nearer to the house he stopped, listened, turned around and ran as fast as he could to his car and backed out of the driveway. That's the story."

"Okay," Geneva said.

"You don't understand. The police never showed up. That salesman thought a murder or torture was taking place and he did nothing. I remember laughing—I was maybe eleven years old and already I had a bitter laugh. What if that was me screaming as I was being knifed to death and that healthy big adult just ran away and didn't do anything? You know what? For the rest of his life that man will feel contempt for himself. For letting a human being die or be beaten. And he'll never know. He'll never know for sure what happened after he heard that screaming, but he'll always know what a contemptible coward he is."

"I should have saved Mira Wallacz," Geneva said. "Is that what your story is about? I'm the salesman who left the scene?"

"It could just as easily have been you who got killed—except you're not famous."

"You don't have to be famous to be killed. It seemed like all the people I noticed at that festival had grudges against Mira Wallacz or at best mixed feelings, the way they referred to her, without compassion. Like if she died it would be interesting and that's all—interesting and in their best interest. That's what I thought back then—that there were people there who didn't want her to turn up alive."

Aida leaned forward. "So you don't believe it was just rocks falling. You believe someone targeted her and tried to make it look like an accident. That's what you think now, right? You know what you have to do, don't you? You have to find that priest again."

"He's not a priest anymore. And he was never very priestly-seeming."

"Right? That should give you hope. You need to find out more about him. First off, why he joined the priesthood and why he left."

"In the beginning he must have wanted to be useful and thought the priesthood was the best avenue for doing that. Obviously it wasn't the right life for him. He didn't know what he needed."

"You make him sound like Maria in *The Sound of Music* before she met that awful stiff-legged fascist Captain Von Trapp. Your priest might be a murderer. That's what I've always thought about Captain Von Trapp."

Geneva put Mira Wallacz's name in the search bar and held her breath. The *New York Times* obituary popped up. The editors had chosen an early photo—a young Mira Wallacz—black haired, dark-eyed, smooth-skinned. Her death was referred to as a mystery: accident or "foul play. Falling rocks or rocks thrown?" A suggestion that local police muffed the investigation, destroying evidence. The language sounded forced, as if whoever wrote the obituary took directions from nineteenth century novels about lost heroines. And then—an advertisement on the right hand side-bar of the webpage, something from the present dug up by the algorithm. A conference devoted to "The Legacy of Mira Wallacz." The event was being held at the same conference center where Mira Wallacz was last seen alive.

Geneva went to bed early and woke at midnight. No way to expunge guilt. Leaving—leaving a woman alone, the way she'd left Mira Wallacz, the way she'd left her own mother years ago. Of course Geneva's mother shouldn't have been left alone. Her weak, ill mother, helpless. Geneva: guilty of being selfish. Going to that party. Leaving with that boy who claimed his parents were on vacation. After midnight the downstairs door rattled. Adult voices called the boy's name. As if Geneva weren't in his bedroom, the boy didn't speak to her, not even to whisper. It took a long time for his folks to go to bed, for Geneva to feel it was safe to hurry, shoes in her hands, down the staircase. A mist in the downstairs twinkling, a strange thickness of adult awareness, even before she touched the bottom step. At home she found her mother on the bedroom floor with the bedsheet twisted beneath her. Three days later, and while alone in the hospital—for Geneva had left the hospital room momentarily—her mother died.

She wasn't blamed, no one would blame her for her mother's death. No one. And so why should she be guilty for leaving Mira Wallacz alone too? The author was a healthy person, a sane, well-balanced person, and how was Geneva to know that the novelist would die? And that the manner of her death could always be questioned.

Yet Geneva could not stop herself from believing something or someone meant to cause harm to Mira Wallacz. She had left the one still-living person she most admired in the world, left her alone to be destroyed.

She pulled the covers back and took a sketchbook off the bedside table. Drawing would calm her nerves. At first, boxes, then circles, then whirlpools. She drew shooting stars and spirals.

It was a sign, Thom Crystl's appearing at that party, although she didn't want to believe in signs. But how else to understand why he came into her life, that they met and were drawn to one another? Knowing who he was now, she couldn't turn away from the possibility of more discoveries. The past ten years had been a long dream of guilt, a repetitive dream, and here was a way to rupture the dream.

An hour later she had a plan—the first step.

She made the reservation before she could change her mind. Thank God, there were rooms available. An ocean view. How lucky was that?

⊬ Chapter Seven

HE NEXT DAY, Saturday, Geneva called Aida to recruit her. "We don't have to attend the actual workshop," she told her friend. "We could just stay at the hotel where it's being held. As paying guests. We could—observe. And then, if things go the way I hope they will, there's a second part to the plan."

"Is it dangerous?" Aida asked. "Geneva, you know I'm counting on it."

Reserving a room at the hotel where Thom Crystl's workshop was held, simply going for a vacation, that was a nice, not entirely outlandish idea. And confronting Thom Crystl there. Drafting him for the second part of her plan—maybe that was an entirely outlandish idea.

Aida was laughing, almost gurgling.

Geneva said, "I can pay your way."

Aida agreed. "That would be great. I'm running low. We're going to have such fun. We're going to haunt this bastard. I forget his last name?"

Geneva reminded her: Crystl. A name that Mira Wallacz might have been tempted to put into a novel.

"That's what he calls himself now? Crystl. His stripper name. If I ever strip I'm going to borrow it. Crystl—like people can see right through him. Or like he breaks easily. We'll strip away illusion and discover truth. No matter what the police said when they cleared him, you're always going to suspect him, aren't you, unless you get to check him out? He seemed too inept at that party to be dangerous—so that's a plus for him. He didn't seem threatening. I mean, he could hardly stay standing. Very noodle-like. Is this guy, Thom Crystl, a good poet?"

"I read some of his poems online. I think he might be."

"That makes him innocent. A good poet won't kill. I bet that's for fiction writers."

After talking with Aida, Geneva opened Mira Wallacz's first novel and came across her own ink markings, brackets around passages. Why had she found it necessary or useful to mark the following?

> That awkward sensation was upon her. Everything happen-
> ing all at once.
>
> The antique doll—its eyelashes like bristles from a child's
> broom.

Or why had she underlined this:

> The clouds stirred, curdled—the words formed in her mind:
> *What the hell*, clear words, clear as a stone in a stream of
> swiftly running water when the sunlight strikes.

Maybe those sentences were underlined because they were mysterious—glimmering in the middle of what otherwise seemed pretty clear, straightforward. Mira Wallacz's characters—the primary ones anyway—hardly had to work to find out the truth. The truth came to them because they were patient and not grasping. The suffering endured in those novels was so unlike life—there was meaning to be discovered, or maybe meaning was thrust upon characters. All the mysteries tied up nicely, the logic secure, a romance fulfilled. It was the same bag of tricks, a quality of timing. The cultivation of your awareness that the sustained threat operating in the novels wouldn't harm you, not you. You, meaning that somehow the reader became the main character. And so you wound up having these adventures where eventually sex came into the plot—gauzy, ghostlike sex that was attractive, especially if you had been disappointed by the sex you knew most about. What Geneva first learned about sex came from Mira Wallacz's novels. And there was something else—the mystery behind the mystery, the way once you closed the novel you wanted to re-experience the plot because you felt you missed something. A secret eluded you. You wanted to start reading the novel again, to bask in the warm welcome that Mira Wallacz created for you while you tried to figure out what you had ignored.

An unlikely woman always figured out the mystery. Not Mrs. Marple with her neighborly wisdom accrued through age and heightened powers of observation, parlayed precisely because she was underestimated. No, Mira Wallacz's primary characters discovered the truth by pretty much doing everything wrong. Not one was a crumpled detective pretending to be inept while turning out to be foxily clever. No, in Mira Wallacz's world you could keep making mistakes, and even so the world opened its secret panels and revealed a glistening heart. You only had to show up and endure and stumble forward and justice was served. You didn't have to be superior. You could be your own inimitable self among every other inimitable self and accept the self you were with all your limitations. Relax into it. Have a little wine at lunch, many glasses of wine in the space of a month. Eat the same after-work bowl of cheerios and keep asking questions and keep turning up. You didn't have to do too much, really. It was like the world wanted to be known. Ached to be known.

Or was Mira Wallacz basically just writing about being lazy?

That's why her novels were called "cozy mysteries." You could be lazy as a reader, really. You gave up your own pretensions and even some of your borders. You felt enveloped by those novels. You felt almost loved.

PART
THREE

» Chapter Eight

P EERING TOWARD THE BEACH from her hotel room balcony, Geneva endured a wave of vertigo. She focused her eyes on the horizon and then, when her vision cleared, on the beach. The day was misty, the ocean gray. In the distance a tall dark-haired figure stood before a group seated in lounge chairs sunk in the sand.

Another wave of vertigo hit and Geneva looked down at her feet, breathed slowly, and tried to listen to Aida go on about how fun it would be to rent a bike.

"You go ahead."

"Okay," Aida said. She was dressed in shorts and a striped green shirt. "You'll be all right?" One of the nice things about Aida: she wasn't offended if you didn't go along with her plans.

She joined Geneva on the balcony and asked, pointing, "Is that him?"

"I can't tell. I don't think so."

"If it's not him, he still has to be around, somewhere—so that you can bump into him accidentally. You know, I've been thinking about the inheritance you said he left to the church. You'd think they'd have enough money in every one of their churches, what with the Vatican. I've been there. Beautiful magnificent stuff. After a while it starts to look junky, all that loot. I was with a crowd and pushed along. Like I was inside an intestine."

The people on the beach were dispersing, walking in that drunken way people manage on sand. Their leader, Geneva saw now with certainty, wasn't Thom Crystl but a younger, skinnier, light-skinned man.

If he wasn't on the beach then Thom Crystl must be with his workshop group somewhere inside the hotel. How could she approach him, supposing she finally managed to run into him? What would she say? *You danced with me at a party and I drove you to your hotel after I sobered up sufficiently. Actually I wasn't really all that drunk I just liked acting drunk and falling down—what an embarrassment. Remember me?*

After Aida left for her bike ride, Geneva decided to explore the hotel, gain a better sense of the place, maybe bump into Thom Crystl. She reminded herself to slow her breathing. Slow breathing plus meditation is the "ticket" for calming nerves—one of the agency's clients recommended repeatedly. He did a one-man show: Samuel Beckett. Geneva had met him for coffee and he kept her waiting both times, which was a joke to him, not to her. She hadn't seen him since. Another performer—a woman in an improv group—recommended frantic arm wind-milling in a private room to alleviate anxiety. "Exhaust yourself first and then use whatever energy you have left."

Geneva took another deep breath. It wasn't helping. At least she had a strategy: run into Thom Crystl as if she wasn't stalking him. Remind him of their meeting and what good feelings she had about that party. Gradually reveal how much they had in common: a beloved writer.

She passed through a lounge and headed toward the corridor beyond the freight elevators. While sitting in a broad-backed couch in the lounge area she listened to voices coming from a conference room. She couldn't make out a single word. Sheets of rain rattled against the window across from her, hitting the patio tables outside. She hoped Aida would make it back from her bike ride soon.

She brushed at her legs. Sand. Someone must have come from the beach and landed on the couch without bothering to towel off.

She flinched when a door was flung open and a woman with black-rimmed eyes, and dressed in very high shorts, stalked out. "Ugh," the woman moaned. Her face contorted. Geneva couldn't tell if the woman was about to cry or laugh.

"Are you okay?" Geneva asked.

The woman sniffled and approached. "These things—I don't know why I signed up. You relive the worst moments of your life and people talk to you about line breaks. It's inhuman. The poet—well, we're all poets, at least potentially—he's not so bad, except he doesn't hold anyone back from saying anything. It's cruel." The woman paused, looked more closely at Geneva and said, "You're not in any of the workshops, are you? You probably have no idea what I'm talking about."

Before Geneva could answer, the woman hurtled away, her satchel bouncing against her hip.

The door opened again and people poured out, maybe as many as twelve. Geneva sat forward, scanning faces.

She was about to give up and leave when Thom Crystl—it was unmistakably the poet—emerged, looking both ways before advancing into the hallway. In daylight she could see him better than she had before. He looked like someone aching for a nap, heavy lidded, lips parted. Thick eyebrows, which made his eyes look defenseless.

He hurried to her, and the heat rose so quickly to Geneva's head that she endured her third bout of dizziness since arriving at the hotel.

"I'm sorry," he said, his head bent, not looking into her face. "I didn't mean to let it get rough in there. I'll talk to everyone tomorrow and see about setting a new tone. I don't blame you for running out. It was my fault. I shouldn't have let it happen. Your poem had some meltingly good lines." He looked up and spluttered to a stop. He had to have found himself lying and couldn't go on. The woman's poem must have been atrocious.

"Meltingly good lines?" Geneva said.

"It's very difficult to write about a cat's death. I mean it's been done and done well—but it's hard. And what I meant by meltingly good—" He stopped himself. "Are you in Abimbola's group? I'm sorry. The workshops are too large. I thought you were . . . It doesn't matter. Or it does matter. Everyone answered the preference sheet for workshops and I scored last or not at all. Even though they gave three choices of workshop leaders. I suppose I sound like I'm confessing."

"You do," she said.

"I'm sorry. I didn't want to offend anyone today."

His politeness sounded like a parody. Like words spoken by someone who for a long time had to mind his manners, weigh and shrink his natural responses. In cultural terms he was very much like a woman. Which probably meant many women desired him.

He excused himself and hurried away.

In the next corridor Geneva snatched a flyer from the floor. It was good to have a complete list of workshop sessions. There might be events open to the public. At any rate, she could find him easily now that she had a schedule.

Only once before in her life had Geneva ever attended a poetry reading, and it was like being scolded by someone with hiccups.

A mustached, pony-tailed man leaned over the microphone to introduce Thom Crystl. He began with a listing of journals where the poet's work had appeared—titles that meant nothing to Geneva. The speaker's slew of adjectives writhed and bumped against one another: *precision* and *associative power* and *violation of linguistic boundaries* and *density of reference* and a *preference for fantasy over agreed-upon reality*. Geneva's neck prickled. Aida squeezed her arm and whispered "Dear god."

By the time Thom Crystl, wearing a black suit with a skinny tie, made his way to the stage from a seat in the third row Geneva was holding her breath. His suit was too large for him, the shoulders drooping, and his striped blue tie insisted on hanging at a diagonal. He looked like an inexperienced assistant to an undertaker.

He nodded without peering at the audience and picked up a half-empty water glass on the podium's edge. Geneva wondered if the glass was left over from another reader's performance. She had the terrible impression that he was too nervous to swallow, that he was drowning up there, that when at last he spoke water would dribble between his teeth.

It was awful, how sympathetic her body was with his. Just nerves, she told herself. Still, a chord vibrated in her chest. Maybe she wasn't alone? Maybe others in the audience felt this way too? And everyone in the audience was going to be made uncomfortable.

His Adam's apple bounced as he set down the glass. He must have spilled water because he was wiping at the podium and then running his hands down his pant legs.

He looked out and above the audience of women.

"Thank you," he said, his voice shaking. "Thank you for—for—for—being here."

Geneva closed her eyes. The nervous impulse to kick the chair in front of her was overwhelming, even though the chair was occupied by a woman with a very attractive blue streak in the back of her hair. Someone was wearing too much perfume, an offensive musk.

She made herself think of other things, letting images rise, memories come forward. That blue streak—a bird she saw last week outside her apartment building—a jay, quarrelsome, greedy. Blue racers. Her mother had seen one of those snakes—"Geneva, they're so fast. This one streaked right across the road. You wouldn't believe it." Blue skies over . . .

Thom Crystl fumbled with his phone and riffled papers. He looked out again at the audience. She could imagine his anxiety cresting. Hopeless, he would read for himself, he would get through this. She supposed by then the audience was invisible to him.

Thom Crystl was reciting. A deer's hoofprint—that was what she was soon seeing. The print filling with rainwater. His voice was quiet, understated, undemanding. He described a stream flowing and the shadow of branches on the water, the "skin drift" of a lily. She couldn't quite catch and hold the images. Everything seen as if through clouds. A calm dream, she told herself. He's giving us a calm dream. One poem focused on a child carrying a long branch of apple blossoms on a school bus and how, for once, the other boys sat silent. No bullying. The branch must have been like a magic wand, she thought, although that wasn't something the poet mentioned.

Abruptly, blinking, he stopped. He was walking to his seat when the applause—appreciative and loud—began.

"Are you okay?" Aida whispered.

"Of course."

"That was a lot to take in. You want some bad wine and pasty cheese? I do."

Geneva didn't, and headed back to their room. She felt like lying down, escaping the women who would be clustering around Thom Crystl. Her instincts had been right; women liked him, possibly out of sympathy?

When Aida returned from the reception she was laughing as soon as she opened the door. "My god, they adore him down there. He's a god to them. I kept thinking, Give me the bucket. I mean, I enjoyed his reading—in a kind of hypnotic way, and he seems authentic. Pure, you know? I just wasn't inspired. At one point I did think about painting the foyer of my apartment a very pale lavender after he read about violets under ice, but still. There were people there at the reception who adore the poor bugger. Even his fidgeting, they liked that. I suppose it makes everyone feel like they have so much more testosterone than they ever realized. He's so— delicate. When he got near the cheese I felt like lifting him up."

"He has to be at least six feet—"

"Height has nothing to do with it. It's all about the perception of vulnerability, and boy does he ever manage that well. I can see why that writer put him into her will and gave him everything. You feel like he needs a transfusion daily or something. He's begging for protection."

"He looks perfectly healthy."

"That's what's so wrong with him. It's like he's wearing his inner world and it covers all of his skin. Like his inner world is inhabited by snow fairies. God, you like him, don't you?"

"He's an even better poet than I thought he was. It just took me a while to get into the spirit of the reading."

"You need the body to appreciate the work. Okay. But you know what? I think that as simple-minded as those poems were—I mean, they were short—they made no sense, not really. He should stick to dancing."

"I thought you said he's not a good dancer."

"He's a great dancer. A great dancer lets the people they're dancing with feel like they can do anything. You were fully authorized to drop to the floor. Slipping away. He basically turned you into syrup. Maybe that was his impact on that writer. He made her slip and she dropped and the rocks did the rest. Sorry. I shouldn't have said that, Geneva. I didn't mean to sound so—"

"I know you didn't."

"She did slip away though—that's true, isn't it?"

›› CHAPTER NINE

WHEN GENEVA HEADED to the lobby to nab a quick cup of coffee from the mobile cafe she heard Thom Crystl's voice.

"I know you," he said, his head tilted, studying her as he approached. "You're in one of the other workshops? I'm sorry about mistaking you yesterday for someone who was in mine."

She paused before she said, "We were at a party together."

She watched as his face changed shape, his eyebrows lifting and his mouth forming a funny little "o."

"I thought it was you," he said. "You looked so familiar. And then I thought—no, it's too unlikely to see you again. You're the woman I thought was named Teresa. But you're not named Teresa, are you? I'm sorry. I can't remember your name—I only remember what I thought you should be called. I apologize. I probably can't apologize enough. Your name—it will come to me." He brushed his hair back from his forehead and said, "It was a great night. With you and your friend."

"She's here."

"Who?"

"Aida, my friend."

He smiled. "The woman with the hobgoblin."

Geneva told herself not to say what was on the tip of her tongue. She heard herself say it anyway. "We have something in common."

"Oh?" He smiled. She grabbed her coffee and together they stepped toward a couch in the lounge across from the registration desk.

After they sat, she said, "Mira Wallacz."

The elevator disgorged a group of men. One of them called out to Thom Crystl who waved and instantly turned back to Geneva and asked. "How did you know her?"

"I was one of the last to see her alive. I was with her right before what happened. I was there in the woods right before—I know about you—about the inheritance."

He leapt up, his eyes darkening. "What are you trying to pull off?" His voice was a whisper-hiss. "You haven't had your pound of flesh yet?"

She was already punching the button for the elevator when he called after her. "You're Geneva, right? Geneva Finch?"

When she saw her friend's face, Aida stopped talking. The two women sat together on the bed across from the television. Geneva drew her knees to her chin. "Thom Crystl does remember us— there's that. He was furious with me. Maybe I'm a coward. I had to get away from him. I suppose he thinks we're here to accuse him of killing Mira Wallacz."

"Aren't we? Maybe he is guilty. And guilty people are dangerous."

"He's not dangerous," Genva said. "The opposite. He sounded angry and that made me get away from him, but now I wonder if maybe he'd be more likely to be killed than just about anyone I ever met."

"You mean that possibly he's very good at covering his tracks and convincing gullible people of his innocence?"

"I'm not gullible," Geneva said. "I'm trusting my instincts."

"Instincts are useless when it comes to dealing with clever people. You can convince yourself of anything, Geneva."

The phone on the nightstand rang. The two women looked at one another. Geneva answered. "We're in 418," she said. "Right. Okay."

She turned to Aida. "He's coming."

"You're kidding me."

"He wants to explain."

"Or kill us."

"He's not going to kill us. I don't think—"

"Maybe just one of us—you maybe. I should leave."

"Don't."

Already, the knock on the door. Geneva whispered to Aida, "He's harmless."

Aida whispered back, "You're terrifying me."

As soon as Thom Crystl entered the room Geneva turned on the desk lamp near the door although the room was already fully illuminated. Aida pulled out a chair for Thom Crystl. He remained standing.

"I want to apologize," he said. "Geneva, I first approached you yesterday, thinking you were one of the people I'd offended in my session. And then today I bothered you again. I started this. The fact that you knew Mira—I don't know what I was accusing you of. You didn't say anything that was wrong. I apologize—for everything. My mind isn't quite where it should be."

He looked past Geneva as if trying to find his mind before he went on. "I don't know why I ever agreed to do another workshop. I should ask the organizers to give everyone in my sessions their money back. But you two, you have nothing to do with that. I remember you both. It was such a great night at that party. I owe you that night. I've thought about it a lot. It was like a dream, a fever dream. A good fever dream. And now you're here. How did I get so lucky?"

Geneva was struck again by the way he talked about himself. Who talked like that? Pretty much insulting himself.

"Do you want anything to drink?" Aida asked, her voice rising with hope. "We could head down to the bar."

"I'm sorry—again," Thom Crystl said. "I can't. They're all down there from my workshop, and I can't face them. I think I'm losing it, to be frank."

Geneva imagined that maybe he was well practiced in detailing his fears and faults, like a comedian would. A standard way to deflect criticism: criticize yourself first.

"Sit down," Aida said, again pushing the desk chair toward him. Finally, he sat.

The three of them were silent until Thom Crystl spoke again. "Why I feel comfortable confessing so much about my inadequacies to both of you I don't know. I guess it's because, Geneva, you know about Mira."

"You know who killed her?" Aida asked.

"It had to be an accident. I realize what people thought at first. I was the only one who stood to gain."

Geneva spoke quickly to exonerate him. "And then you gave everything to your parish and you left the church and changed your name and became what you've always wanted to be? A poet?"

Aida put up her hands. "I'm ordering from room service. Let's not let our stomachs get all watery." She cautioned Thom Crystl, "Don't say another word. I want to hear everything." She picked up the phone and dialed. "What's your room number?" she asked him.

She repeated the number into the phone and then took the phone into the hallway. After she returned she said, "I ordered us some gin and tonics and fish sandwiches and extra fries." She nodded at Thom Crystl. "I hope you don't mind that I put it on your room bill."

"No," he said. "I like that."

"I thought you would," she said.

Thom Crystl turned to Geneva. "You look like Mira, you know that? When I saw you at that party I thought you were her. Impossible, I know. She's been gone for so long. I was stunned when I saw you. Did you know who I was then?"

"No. I googled. I found out about—the priesthood, your leaving it. And a while ago I read the article that mentioned you. The article in that magazine? I was in that article too—I was the last person to talk to Mira. Did you know about that? Did you know who I was when I told you my name? You read the article that mentioned both of us?"

He sucked in his lower lip. "Can I ask you something? What was Mira acting like when you saw her?"

Geneva was struck by the oddity of the question. She came to the hotel to learn about Thom Crystl's relationship with Mira Wallacz and to make a request. Now he was trying to find out more about the day she had encountered Mira Wallacz. Possibly he had as many questions as she did.

Geneva answered carefully, deciding to leave out the sensations of terror she experienced before she grasped Mira Wallacz's hand. "She wanted me to leave her alone, to go back to the conference center and not tell anyone about seeing her. I've played those moments over again and again, and it only becomes blurrier. I'm not sure if remembering each time adds another layer, and if I'm beginning to misremember what happened. I didn't know her—I came to the festival because I wanted to meet her. I loved her novels, worshipped them. They helped me. But you—how did you know Mira?"

Thom Crystl paused. Geneva could tell he was making a decision that was difficult for him. Finally, he said, "We were neighbors. She was always giving my brother and me cookies when we were kids. She took an interest in us both. She wasn't happy when I entered the seminary. She wrote to me. A pretty blistering letter. Later I confess that I thought I could help her—arrogant, I know. She began confiding in me. She was a clever woman. I confess—"

"You like to say you confess, don't you?" Aida said.

"It's a habit. The fact is, I had tried to get her to think about her spiritual life. I admit contacting her a few times, hoping I could be helpful. After her identity was revealed, she sent me her novels when each came out. I thought it was nostalgia—she remembered me as a kid, someone to give treats to. Sending me her books seemed like an extension of that generosity. The novels, to me they appeared to be a record of how she was searching for something that wasn't in this world. I think it was just an idiosyncrasy of hers—to put me in the will. Probably she didn't intend to keep me in her will. Anyway, I should go. I just wanted to apologize."

"You're not going," Aida said. "I ordered for all of us."

"I don't quite feel like I'd be good company."

"Since when has that mattered? You were never especially good company at that party and Geneva still remembers you."

Geneva's heart was in her throat. Now or never—the words kept repeating in her mind. Changing to *now and never and never and now*.

She leaned toward Thom Crystl. "You would like justice for Mira, wouldn't you? That's important, isn't it? Justice."

"It was never entirely clarified—what exactly happened. It was an accident though, that's what was finally determined."

"I don't believe it was an accident."

"There was no proof it was anything other than an accident." His eyes shifted from Geneva's. He twisted away from her in his chair, then twisted toward her again.

She said, "You know that there's a conference in October devoted to her memory. You've heard about the conference?"

"I donated to that," he said. "But I'm not attending."

Aida murmured, "I knew you didn't give all that money to the parish."

Thom Crystl went on. "The conference is put on by a group that's basically a fan club. They didn't have much in the way of funds. They don't need me there. I have no intention of attending."

"But you want justice for Mira?" Geneva said.

"I don't understand."

"Mira Wallacz may have been murdered. You have to realize that. Until you were cleared you were a suspect, as was I—because I was with her there where—"

"No one would have wanted to harm Mira."

Was he lying? He had to be. Or maybe he was too innocent, too pure to know much about envy, too removed from reality. Geneva's voice rose. "You can't believe that no one wanted anything to happen to her. I remember the participants at that festival, the way they talked about her. I was there. I saw and heard. And now there's a chance, it's only a chance, that maybe there's a way to know more about what happened. I've already checked the program for this year's conference. A few of those people who were there ten years ago are returning. They were excited about the possibility of Mira vanishing. I'm haunted by the possibility that she was killed. Aren't you?"

He ran his hands over his face. When he finally spoke he said, "Sometimes. Sometimes I am."

She felt a flush of triumph. She had led him to this moment, led him to agreeing with her.

"We should do more than just wallow around wondering about what happened to her," she said.

She described her plan: the two of them could announce that they were editing a collection of writings about Mira Wallacz—appreciations, short memoir-like pieces by critics and writers influenced by her. Because Thom had a reputation as a poet their proposal to edit a collection would be taken seriously. At the conference they could interview any of the people who agreed to talk to them.

Thom Crystl was silent, staring forward.

"I bet they'll all talk to you," Aida said to him. "Sorry I can't be there. Sounds like fun. They're never going to suspect that you think one of them, or more than one, is a murderer. You both seem so clueless."

"I am, at any rate," Geneva said. She looked at Thom Crystl. "I do need help. I really do need your help."

Thom glanced from Geneva to Aida and back again. "Why would I want to do what you're proposing?"

Geneva kept her voice steady. "If a person involved in her death is one of the participants who was at the original festival they might be back. How could they resist? They wanted to destroy her, and now her legacy is stronger than ever. Maybe they want to dispute that. They want to confirm what they believed—that she didn't deserve respect or to live. I know I'm sounding melodramatic. But think: it will help me at least to try to find out more. Not knowing—and wondering if my instincts are wrong—that's been—more of a struggle than I can even begin to explain. You're a writer—it will be your sort of environment. It will seem legitimate for you to be at the conference. Because we can say we're working on a collection of essays about Mira Wallacz we'll have an excuse to interview some of those people."

Thom Crystl said, "You're willing to lie."

"If you do edit a collection of essays we won't be lying. You should edit a collection about her, right? You owe Mira Wallacz that much, maybe? Or more? We could talk to some of the same people who were there in the past—they'll be on panels, at least a couple of them. The program's on the website."

He was studying the curtains stretched over the mammoth window. "Why would they let us interview them?" he asked.

Geneva cocked her head, willed him to look at her. When he met her gaze she said, "I think you're not really listening to me. They'll talk to us because you'll say we're editing a collection. You're a poet. They probably know that—not your connection to Mira Wallacz. That's still secret, unless someone does some very advanced online searching, I guess."

"So what we'd be attempting, actually, in your imagination, would have some legitimacy?"

"I wouldn't rule it out."

"Why not do this without me?"

"As I'm suggesting, you'll make it sound legitimate. You're a writer, I'm not. You knew Mira Wallacz. Because you knew her you'll understand things that I won't." She paused before she said, "You're like me more than you realize."

Had she gone too far? He shook his head, confused. She went on, "You suffer too because of Mira. How could you avoid it? We both have suffered for years. Wondering about what happened. I just need help. I really need your help." Her words had rushed out before Aida could interrupt, Aida who hated to see Geneva lowering herself, begging.

"Let me think about it."

"You have to think about it?"

"I have to think, Geneva."

"You'll consider it—carefully?"

As Thom Crystl left the room, Aida said, "Someone's taking an awful long time with room service."

After the poet left and his footsteps couldn't be heard in the hall, Aida was the first to speak. "I don't believe him."

"I'm not sure I do either. He's keeping something back."

"People always do." Aida ran her hand through her hair before she said, "I don't know why you think you need him. You had to sound like fucking Nancy Drew to get him to listen to you. Wheedling. You were wheedling. You really might be better without him. Who is he anyway? Why do you think he quit the priesthood? Maybe it was about a woman: Mira Wallacz? She was, what—about fifty or fifty-five? I'm guessing he would have been around thirty when she died. That's kind of a perfect age spread. I bet he feels guilty because she gave him everything. He was a priest. Guilt, that's their job."

"I identify with his guilt—for leaving Mira Wallacz alone. I was afraid—"

"You were right to be afraid. It could have been you."

"It wouldn't have been. No one knew me. No one cared."

"You're saying you weren't worth murdering."

"Absolutely."

"Geneva, murderers don't need a reason."

"Maybe this one did. "

Room service arrived at last. Geneva changed the number on the check to her own room number.

"Are you sure?" Aida said. "That guy really does owe you. For that poetry reading alone."

"If only he believed he owed me something," Geneva said. "That would make things so much easier."

⊁ CHAPTER TEN

AIDA WAS STILL ASLEEP when Geneva slipped out. If all else failed she'd be able to say she breathed ocean air and hadn't been cooped up, paranoid and suspicious. Not for the entire weekend anyway.

She walked the beach, her shoulders wrapped in a long scarf. The light was already dazzling. A woman called to her, waving her over. Geneva recognized her: it was the woman who ran out of Thom Crystl's workshop yesterday. That was how life so often worked: the person you didn't want to see will materialize before your eyes, a rule almost harder to escape than gravity.

The woman sat cross-legged. On her blanket was settled a large beach bag from the top of which peaked a notebook. Geneva imagined the woman intended to write while on the beach, that she was there for inspiration.

When Geneva arrived in front of her, the woman scanned her, gazing at the loose linen pants Geneva wore, the white blouse skimming her hips. "I have a question," she said. "How do you know Thom? I saw you sitting with him yesterday in the lobby. You're not in my workshop. You let me think you were."

"You assumed I was in the workshop, that was all. Thom and I met not long ago—at a party."

The wind picked up sand. The woman pushed a strand of hair from her face and squinted. "I was just wondering if he's in a relationship."

"I don't know. I can't answer that question. Even if I knew."

"Well, thanks anyway," the woman said, her tone sour.

Geneva made a guess: this person fled the workshop to gain Thom Crystl's attention. She was accustomed to being followed out of a room. And Thom—he was exceptionally attractive to women, that was once again amply evident. Who wouldn't be attracted to him? Was Mira Wallacz attracted to him, as Aida had guessed?

An hour later when Thom Crystl called the phone in her room Geneva was glad Aida was getting a pre-lunch drink in the downstairs bar. It was easier to concentrate without interruptions.

"I should give you my cell phone number," she said.

"It's all right."

"You mean you're not going to ever talk to me again?"

"Geneva, I'm calling because I have some questions. Before— or if—I agree to go with you to the conference I need to know more. Okay?"

"Certainly."

"Staff people might remember me, some might even be former parishioners."

"That should be all right," Geneva said. "You're not denying who you are. If local people recognize you they should be sympathetic—you gave your inheritance to the parish. And Mira Wallacz must have been a local celebrity. They had to have admired her and must admire you too."

"Local people knew Mira, plenty of them, and for the most part they disliked her. They thought she got 'above herself,' as some of them would say. Bingle's the kind of town where if you diverge from what's expected you're putting on airs."

"Aren't they sympathetic now, given what happened to her?"

"People think she was the victim of loose soil on a high slope and it was just bad luck for her to be traipsing around and not realize that rocks can fall on your head. We're not known for curiosity or empathy in my home town."

"Maybe we should widen the possible suspects and include townspeople?"

"You really are talking about suspects." His tone was incredulous.

"Yes, suspects. We have a right to be suspicious."

His breathing echoed in the phone before he said, "I don't want to seem like I'm cynical, play-acting friendliness when you want us to suspect every single person we see."

"I haven't said that directly, but yes, let's suspect everyone. Why not? We want justice. And I've been haunted for too long. You weren't at the festival ten years ago. You were cleared. And now that I've met you, knowing who you are, you're doubly cleared. Plenty of others, though, weren't investigated by the police—to my knowledge."

"Supposing it wasn't an accident—and that's a wild speculation," he said, "I still can't believe it. Was there any single person at the festival that you most suspected back then while you were there? Someone you told the police about?"

"I didn't want to bear false witness. I was pretty naive, admittedly. Some of the people I overheard didn't like her, I knew that, but I didn't think it was right to speculate to the police about people I didn't even know. Although I used to think it could be like that Agatha Christie novel and they all had a hand in her murder."

Thom Crystl cleared his throat. "I'll admit it was uncanny, her death. There were falling rocks every season. Probably one rock hit another rock and glanced off that rock and gravity did the rest. Maybe you're on a fool's errand, Geneva. The case was pretty much given up. Just a freakish thing. What about people remembering you? Won't they remember you were there at the festival?"

"Ten years ago I was shy and invisible. I don't think anyone will remember me."

"Hard to believe."

Mira went ahead with the question she most wanted to ask. "Had you known you were going to inherit—"

"I had no idea."

"You really did give everything to your parish?"

"It seemed the right thing to do."

"Is that what Mira would have wanted?"

"There's no way to know that, is there?" Irritation entered his voice. "None of this should have ever become public information. The fact that I was named executor and inheritor came out, but that has never been challenged. No one had the right to question Mira's judgment. She didn't often explain herself anyway."

Geneva felt her own irritation rising. "Someone who was at that conference has always known more than they're telling. Don't you think that's the case? Am I just imagining all this? I remember that there was that biographer back then and she seemed delighted that Mira was missing. For sales of the biography she planned to write."

"Tama Squires? I read the biography."

"Me too. It's awful. A travesty. She gave so much about you away—but not your name."

"She interviewed me over the phone before I changed my name. I never met with her in person to discuss Mira."

"That's good. She won't recognize you. Anway, she exonerated you. You were saying Mass."

"Anyone else at the festival who looked guilty to you?"

"Another woman—I can't remember her name this instant, Luisa something or other, she's in this year's program again. She kept saying how much she admired Mira and pressed on that idea too hard, like she was trying to convince herself. And then there was Mira's agent who was vilified because she didn't keep Mira's identity secret. She was at the festival too. Back then I just caught a glimpse of her, that was all, but she's worth talking to. You agree that we should meet them, talk to them? Oh—and an old friend of Mira's was there—I almost forgot about her, and the way she talked about Mira Wallacz suggested she envied her."

"You must have spent most of your time eavesdropping."

"I couldn't help but hear the envy in their voices."

"Lots of people are envious. But they don't kill anyone. I'm still—thinking." He was silent for far too long before going on. "I have another question: What did you do that afternoon right before you went into the woods and found Mira?"

"I didn't want to stay back in my room, even though my roommate had left by then. The panels were on a break or maybe just about over, most of them, for the afternoon. I didn't really have a plan, other than wanting to get out of the building, but part of me— I admit—thought I could find Mira, that I could be a hero. And the woods looked beautiful."

She felt the temptation to walk among the trees when she was first let off from the bus and headed up the road toward the conference center. The trees, the leaves dry and creaking high in the air, heaving with each gust. She was reminded of how she comforted herself when her mother was ill. She would run behind the house into the woods, crouch by the stream, reeds brushing her shoulders. She would know she had escaped for only a short time, know that she would have to run back to the house to help her mother. But for a while she could vanish—disappear into the living, moving, green and gold world where no one needed her. Back then, when she looked up into the trees she told herself they were guarding her the same way when, as a very young child, she gathered fallen bark and made stick houses, imagined that she could invite an invisible, protective friend, smaller than her wrist, to live in such houses.

Thom Crystl said, "It must have felt good when you first caught sight of Mira."

"It felt wonderful." She paused before she said, "Until I felt something else, like we were being watched. I couldn't make out if it was even human, what was watching us. I grabbed her hand like a maniac and ran with her."

"You ran with her?"

"I know. I was frightened and took her hand and we ran."

"It's funny that she let you."

"It was funny. It's as if we knew each other. I knew her from her writing. She couldn't have known me."

A prickle of alarm ran over Geneva's neck. Was she telling him the full truth about how she found Mira? She remembered a poem—something about how we run to what we fear. What had transpired after Mira Wallacz dismissed her? She could remember, foggily, turning back toward the conference center. Later, the shock of hearing what happened to the author—the shock blotted out so much for Geneva, and now made her memories suspect.

All the little sensory reminders were only what remained— light sifting through the trees, the warm sliding sweatiness of Mira's hand in her own, and then the light dimmed and she was alone again, alone and hurrying, with a secret. And the woods, breathing with their own secrets.

"Why do you think someone who attended that festival all those years ago had to be the murderer—if a murder was committed? Maybe a stranger accidently dislodged stones and one struck Mira and that person is never going to come forward."

"Thom, I felt it—a sort of malevolence at that conference. I'll always regret leaving her. I could have stayed in the woods with her. I could have watched from a safe distance. And intervened. Or if it was an accident I could have been a witness and got help. I don't know how long she was lying there. Maybe there was time. And there's something else. The stone that hit Mira and the other stones found around her body—I dream about those. In the dreams I see a hand, it's wrapped in something, something dark blue, and the hand isn't large. It's a woman's hand."

"Dreams are not reliable."

"I know," she said. "But for someone who at least for a time believed in the importance of the soul you're being awfully frustrating."

She ended the call first.

Thom Crystl would come with her to the conference, Geneva told herself. There was something about him that was—suggestible. He would follow her suggestions.

The air coming off the balcony was fresh, scrubbed clean by yesterday's rain.

She went online to the conference website. Listed on the online program were talks about Mira Wallacz's influence on new generations of writers, on the gender fluidity of her novels, on the subversive strategies her work waged upon the more conventional novels in her subgenre. And more. Mira Wallacz as "The Purveyor of the Woozy Mystery." A panel devoted to "the anonymous years" and another to "the identity years." A panel tasked with comparing Mira Wallacz to Jane Austen and Zadie Smith. Another titled "The

Cheaper Elena Ferrante and *The Valley of the Teacups"*—about Mira Wallacz's first novel, written before Ferrante's most popular novels appeared. Although Mira Wallacz was being claimed for academics, most of the people who would be in attendance, Geneva was willing to bet, were strictly admirers, general readers, people like herself.

She pulled out her tattered copy of the old festival program and cross-listed participants with the online listing for the upcoming conference. She checked names online with photographs to be sure her memory was correct. Yes, Tama Squires, once again, was a headliner. Two years after Mira Wallacz's death, Geneva had forced herself to read the biography, scanning quickly the account of ambiguous circumstances surrounding Mira Wallacz's death. Then tossing the book in a donation bin. Another headliner: the novelist Luisa Chaudette. Ten years ago at the lake she hadn't quite believed the novelist's praise for Mira Wallacz. She wondered if Luisa Chaudette still sounded guilty when she talked about the novelist. Also in the program: Stephanie Binks, the agent, controversial for outing Mira Wallacz's identity. She was offering pitch sessions for an extra fee, allowing emerging writers a chance to be signed on for representation. The chance for that approval was no doubt low or non-existent: Geneva recalled Stephanie Binks's apparently bad temper, her hissing of Mira Wallacz's name and her dismissal of that other woman—Inger something or other. She double-checked the festival program. In the old program Inger Delft was one of the speakers—it had to be the same woman. Geneva checked the online form for the upcoming conference: no Inger appeared in the line-up of speakers. Then too, there had been a person at the lake claiming she was Mira Wallacz's friend ever since childhood. Her name, if Geneva ever caught it, had flown from memory. No other names from the first festival brochure were listed. It didn't matter,

Geneva told herself. At the conference she could force herself to be gregarious and meet people. She just needed to grow another, thicker layer of skin.

She sent emails, identifying herself as Thom Crystl's assistant and appended information about him—his recent publications in *The Atlantic* and *The New Yorker*. She could never do this without him, she believed. Or at least she would find it impossible to prove she had any connection to literary culture. That old research paper on Marianne Moore's tricorn hat wouldn't suffice.

And then, the inevitable doubt . . . What had she done? What made her think she could just go ahead with the emails when Thom Crystl hadn't agreed to help her?

And what if it all went wrong? She could find, if Thom Crystl even agreed to accompany her, that their quest was for nothing, and he would quietly disappear from her life. She would return to her old life with nothing gained except embarrassment.

Did she actually think anyone at the upcoming conference would, somehow, in some way, confess to her? Just because ten years had elapsed and the murderer had never been caught and probably felt invincible, did Geneva think they would now admit to a killing? Or maybe brag? No, she couldn't hope for anything like that. And were any of the women she remembered capable of murder? That biographer, Tama Squires—even a decade ago she didn't look strong enough to throw many actual stones. Insults, maybe, not stones. Although she imagined that even Tama Squires, if enraged, might have found the strength to hurl just the right, deadly rock.

What Geneva had to hope for: one person would say something, some little thing. And she'd know. The crack in their story would appear and she could watch truth squirm into the light.

And when again would there be a gathering like the ten-year anniversary conference in memory of Mira Wallacz? The notices online made the conference sound more like a festival than anything more serious. People would let their guards down. For all she knew, the celebration would turn out to be the final opportunity to discover what happened to Mira Wallacz.

If he had any imagination at all, Thom Crystl should understand how much she was haunted. He should understand that by embarking on this seemingly hopeless quest she could at least temporarily quiet the guilty ghost of memory that woke her at night, that reached for her hand and wouldn't let go.

In a half hour she received a text from Thom Crystl.

One word, two letters: OK.

PART
FOUR

⋙ CHAPTER ELEVEN

VINES BRISTLED on the pillars near the entrance, nearly obscuring the stone faces. To her left the stone face looked nearly the same as it had years ago. To her right the nose on the stone face had been bobbed. The face conveyed an air of jolly, chilly indifference to decay.

The potted palms on the walkway were new, as well as the patio chairs arranged in circles. The lobby sofas were red and black, not white like Geneva remembered. On the nearest wall, in gold frames, dozens of brides were photographed holding bouquets, advertising the center's attraction as a wedding venue. Geneva craned to look into a ballroom. The parquet was scuffed, but the white columns looked pristine. A shimmering silver curtain covered a wall, conveying what must have been the designer's stab at elegance.

Geneva was sure the woman on the couch farthest from the entrance, her hair dyed dandelion yellow, was the same woman she saw a decade ago. Someone who sat in the lounge quietly reading, in the exact posture as today. Two of the other women milling about among about a dozen others also looked familiar, only aged a little. How dreamlike, Geneva couldn't help but think, how strange that she was back in the conference center after all this time. And then the possibility emerged, a bubble of a thought: someone might die again. An absurd thought she dismissed.

A table held stacks of Mira Wallacz's novels, new editions with new covers, bold purples and reds and yellows—geometric designs, without human presences. Amid the sharp angles were blots, as if a cat stepped in ink and sprinted across the books. Geneva's own copies from previous decades usually featured a white woman or a pale bluish unreal figure in deep shadow. Often, too, the suggestion of flowers in a foggy background. Or a halo of flowers around a human figure. Those covers were so shiny they looked decoupaged, glossy as hard candy. She picked up a reissue of *Time Flown*. A series of interlocking arrows on the cover. Deckle edged pages. Blots. The book looked thicker, more prosperous than the copy back in her apartment.

On a separate table she discovered a pile of the title released after Mira Wallacz's death: *The Green Man's Smile*. A reissue, a cover in shades of green: forest green, a near lime, and in diagonals, a face that was almost a human's, almost a horse's. Across the front spread a gilt-edged banner: Uncanny Masterwork. And on the back cover: "The plot of Wallacz's last novel predicted her death with bizarre accuracy." When Geneva set the book back her fingers left wet marks and her stomach twisted. She told herself that as long as she didn't read the author's final book there was something still unfinished about Mira Wallacz, still waiting. For all she knew, her own failure to save Mira Wallacz could be coded in the book. Maybe anyone would say she was being ridiculous, but she feared she would relive the horror of the author's death with each page.

Geneva's hotel room was immense—she'd paid for that. Like a gift to her younger self, to prove she didn't have to live the way she used to. She would never be the poor girl who had to take the charity bunk and room with a sad elderly stranger. Never again wander around and snatch up a stale doughnut abandoned hours earlier. She was fully employed with a stable job—maybe a job where she represented people who had little to no stability, true, but even if her bank account was low, generally she was solvent.

The bedspread: a field of lilies. The room even smelled of lilies.

She was lying on the bed, flat on her back when Thom Crystl texted to see if she had arrived and if he could stop by to talk. She gave him her room number and drew from her satchel a list of questions for each person who, over email, had agreed to an interview.

"We don't need to work with predetermined questions," Thom Crystl said, pulling out a desk chair to sit opposite her. "We can make it simple. Ask them what they'd like to contribute to the volume. The less prepared we are the more authentic we'll sound."

"How can that be?"

"Obviously you don't know academics. Listen, Geneva, I've agreed to help you. Because you need—closure. I'll talk to every person here if it gives you closure."

"You don't need closure too?"

"I don't know that I believe in closure."

She handed him interview times, cell numbers. "You're very organized," he said.

"It wasn't much work. Hardly anyone responded. We can talk people into giving us an interview once we meet more of them at the reception—maybe everyone will be there for that."

"You can represent us at the reception. Listen, I'm not going to lie to people. I can't ethically. I'm having more second thoughts than I realized I would."

"We won't lie. We'll just ask questions."

Already Geneva missed Aida. The two of them had nothing in common, except work, although their methods at the agency differed widely. But who else could she pour her heart out to—even if half the time Aida wasn't listening?

"You should be here," Geneva said as soon as her friend answered her phone. "Thom Crystl is terrible. Unprepared. He isn't even interested in the questions I wrote up. Now I don't know why he agreed to come."

"I do," Aida said. "For you it's about murder. For him it's about— you. I have to go. I'm late already. Remember, you can pull this off. With or without Thom Crystl. He must think it's all like a game you're playing and so he can play along, that's all."

"He's humoring me?"

"Not very well, obviously. He's not that optimistic. Maybe he's right not to prepare too much. It's easy to get people to talk. Our species climbed out of trees just so we could dictate our memoirs. You can't fail."

Women were arrayed in groups or picking up plates at the reception buffet in the ballroom. The majority who were milling about were at least two decades older than Geneva. Some had found friends and were seated at tables. Laughter rolled through the south end of the ballroom. Mira Wallacz's true readers were happy to have found one another.

She headed toward a neglected portion of the buffet. Prof-
iteroles. A warm empty shell. Like biting into air, plus a consisten-
cy—eggy—and then the wonder of whipped cream. She moved next
toward a vegetable platter, with carrots, celery, radish roses and
one of those bouquets with sliced apples and cantaloupe and pears
on sticks, fruit that looked overly handled, no thanks.

She saw, with relief, Thom coming through the entrance. His
face shone with what appeared to be self-consciousness and embarrassment. How had he ever convinced himself years ago that he
could be a priest? And yet there was something ethereal, vaguely
spiritual, about him, his feet not quite touching parquet.

She was bumped from behind and a woman, wearing a beret,
apologized at length. Geneva scanned the room. Tama Squires
should be easy to spot. Unless she had changed dramatically, she'd
be pup-tented in a caftan and talking louder than anyone else.

When Geneva gave up on finding Tama Squires, she looked
again for Thom and couldn't find him. She realized, not much later,
that he must have taken a few steps into the room, turned, and fled.

She picked up her plate, careful not to let broccoli spears slide,
perilously at the plate's rim. At least she was having better luck
than another woman. Parts of a fish taco, the interior, were dripping down the woman's dress. It took Geneva a moment to realize
she was staring at Luisa Chaudette, who dabbed at her chest before
backing out of the room.

The thought flashed through Geneva's mind: had Luisa
Chaudette backed out when she saw that Thom Crystl left? Did
Luisa Chaudette want to talk to him? Did they know one another?

The voice came from behind her. "You were pointed out to me."
Geneva recognized Mira Wallacz's agent, hardly unchanged in ten
years. A tiny, furious-looking person. "You and somebody or other,
a poet, are putting together a book about Mira."

Geneva reached over and set her plate on a nearby table. "Yes, it will be a collection of essays, appreciations, reflections."

Stephanie Binks's face hardened. "You're not going to be the first."

Geneva took a guess. "You're writing something?"

When the agent didn't answer Geneva said, "We won't be in competition with you if you're putting a book out. We're just planning something small. In fact, I wrote to you. By email. We hope you'll contribute."

"I never saw the email."

The room was growing louder with voices. A scraping sound. Someone must be moving a chair near Geneva, close to her heels. Yet she couldn't draw her gaze away from the agent.

"Maybe I will contribute," Stephanie Binks said, at last looking less enraged.

"Can we talk tomorrow—when things are quieter?" Geneva asked.

"All right." The agent looked down before giving Geneva a brilliant smile. They agreed on a time to meet in the lobby. Geneva was about to back away when she heard Thom Crystl's voice. He stretched out his hand, introducing himself to Stephanie Binks.

"So you're the poet," she said. "I read something by you—once. I can't remember where I saw it. And so now you're putting together a collection about Mira. Her reputation has only gotten stronger, her posthumous reputation. Her reputation while she was living— I had something to do with creating a readership for her, and I suppose you must know that."

"It had to be fascinating to work with her," Thom Crystl said.

Stephanie Brinks smiled—a warm smile. "You have no idea," she said, her voice low.

She drifted away.

Thom Crystl was staring after the agent's retreating form, her sinuous steps, her admirable posture. Stephanie Binks is a thoroughly unlikeable person who believes she's charming, Geneva was tempted to tell him.

When they were headed to their rooms she asked, "Where were you earlier? I saw you come in and then dart back out." She thought he had abandoned her.

"It was just— I had to deal with my nerves. And then I realized that none of the locals on staff remembered me. Or would admit it anyway. I've apparently changed. Plus, years ago the first thing they noticed was the collar. Not my face."

"You always wore a collar?"

"Often enough. Anyway, I forced myself to come back in. I thought I was here to help you calm your mind, but I'm the one having the most trouble."

She laughed. "You're with me to calm my mind? You can forget about that. It's not happening." How was it possible, people—including elderly people—ever called this man "Father"? Brother, maybe.

In her hotel room she finished a mini wine bottle and a stash of chocolates and pulled back the bed's coverlet. She read a while—which usually helped her to sleep. It wasn't working. She'd be a wreck without sleep. There was no way around it. Something was keeping her up. Already she felt like she was missing a vital clue, maybe about Mira Wallacz, and maybe about her own life.

⸻ CHAPTER TWELVE

B EFORE THE INTERVIEW with Stephanie Binks there was time to
attend a panel presentation. Geneva settled on "Narcissists
in Mira Wallacz's Fictions: Taxonomies." What she knew: narcissism was about power over others through reputation manage-
ment, which sounded, frankly, like her job at the agency.

The first speaker worked in counseling and claimed she drew
her conclusions from her clients, multiple web searches, and common sense. Geneva pulled out a pen to take notes and jotted the
following:

> Self-destroying narcissist—prefers to be seen as a victim to
> gain attention in all situations. Vengeful.
>
> Virtuous narcissist—seeks to be seen as pure and good in all
> situations. Vengeful.
>
> Compelling narcissist—derives power from extreme per-
> suasion/changing others' views of themselves in all situa-
> tions. Vengeful.
>
> Self-righteous narcissist—aligns self-image with a cause,
> and the cause becomes the all-consuming self in all situ-
> ations. Vengeful.

Can't there be narcissists who are all four types? Like: "everything narcissists." Geneva believed she could have added a few
types to the list. Her job experience proved it. But vengeance

hadn't been the motive of many of the agency's clients. The thing about being an artist of the sorts she worked with, they were thirsty for admiration and they were vulnerable. She nearly felt love for some of them. There had to be a category of narcissism that was only about survival rather than revenge. According to each repetitive panelist, Mira Wallacz created a taxonomy of narcissists among the murderers she wrote about.

At any rate, Geneva thought she and Thom should consider if anyone they talked to at the conference had vengeance as a motive for murder. It seemed like vengeance might be a secret motive. But what self-respecting narcissist would admit to it?

After Geneva and Thom approached Stephanie Binks in the lobby the agent announced that they should conduct the interview outside. Already she was giving the impression that she hardly had time for either Geneva or Thom, that she simply wanted company during a cigarette break.

They headed to the lawn at the rear of the center, past the lower parking lot. The day was overcast and Geneva wished she brought her jacket. The wind was coming up, rippling the tops of long grasses on a stretch sloping toward what looked like marshland. Once all three were settled in Adirondack chairs Stephanie Binks lit the cigarette she'd been dangling in her right hand. She crossed and uncrossed her legs and tugged at her jacket.

Geneva repeated information in the email she'd sent earlier. The deadline for submissions, format. Contract details to be worked out after a publisher was secured. She hoped what she said sounded legitimate. She was bored by listening to herself—maybe that would make the offer sound real.

"Any questions?" Geneva asked. "We hope you'll contribute. That's why we wanted to meet you. To convince you."

"No need to convince me, not entirely."

When Thom Crystl didn't say anything and the silence grew awkward, Geneva asked, "What was Mira Wallacz's relationship like with the majority of her readers, as you understood it?"

Stephanie Binks dropped her hand over the side of the chair and stubbed out her cigarette in the grass. "She got the most ludicrous letters and insisted I forward them all to her. I was always the first point of contact. Letters about how she corrupted children. How she was condemned to hell for eternity. How she hated all men. Some of her books were banned in stupid backward places. You probably noticed—everyone notices it now, but not until after I pointed it out in an interview: she never lets a woman become a murderer. And the man in the end is revealed to be a godawful, unrepentant psychopath. Gendered, binary plots. Some people thought that was because she couldn't stand men, although that couldn't be farther from the truth. Did they tell you she was struck in the temple? A person dies in mysterious circumstances quite often in her novels. Ironic, as if she intuited her fate. Or sought it."

Geneva glanced at Thom Crystl, who stared ahead, unblinking. She asked, "You thought she wanted to die?"

"I did. I thought, truly, she wanted to kill herself. That possibly she even thought about hiring someone to do it for her, out of the blue. Maybe to keep her work alive—the way dead authors have the best careers. Everybody buys up the work and then all the posthumous crap comes out. Very lucrative. You could publish a grocery list if it came from someone who achieved notoriety and was safely dead. I worried that she went into those woods looking for someone to harm her, and with her luck she did find a way to die—by falling rocks. She always had a way of making things work out the way she wanted. Nothing was taken for granted."

Geneva bristled. "You disliked her, didn't you?" She regretted her words instantly.

Stephanie Binks shook her head. "No. Certainly not. I didn't know her well enough to dislike her, even though I represented her for years. She was such an unusual person. She practiced a tricky level of deception. I wasn't her literary executor. Did you know that? She chose a—a priest."

Geneva made sure not to look at Thom Crystl before she asked, "You thought you were her executor and didn't know whom she named?"

"I hope you're not suggesting I was glad about what happened, expecting an inheritance. I loved her, in my own way. Though I did feel manipulated by her. I loved her, for her flaws, for being who she was. It wasn't reciprocated, apparently. I would have been an excellent executor. The priest handed her wealth over to his god-forsaken congregation."

Geneva waited for Thom Crystl to say something before she asked, "You'll be writing a piece about what it was like to work as Mira's agent?"

"I haven't committed myself to your project yet, have I? If I do write something it might be about what it was like to discover Mira."

Thom stretched forward, nodding his head. "You're hoping to set the record straight?" he said.

"Maybe." Stephanie Binks shook out a cigarette from a pack she pulled from the crocheted bag at her feet. "I don't know if many people will understand. Despite the inevitable frustrations, I did have fun. Lots of it. It was a challenge. I helped her with her plots—no one knows about that. I just had to suggest a few essential things to her and then, gradually, she developed my idea into a plot. The originating ideas, those were always mine. She was a trance writer—going deeply into her own mind. First, a seed had to be planted. That was one of my gifts, always, ever since I was a child. A special gift. I've always been very good at coming up with suggestions. I was used, frankly. But all good things have to come to an end."

"Why did you reveal her identity?" Geneva asked.

Stephanie Binks blew out smoke, drew in her breath, and wiped something from her shirt. "She never told me not to. It wasn't even a tacit agreement. After a while it became a moral problem. It seemed immoral to lie. And it became tiring covering for her. Plus, it wasn't as if her writing would suffer if people knew who she was. Once her identity was revealed her career really took off. She made good use of being known too—creating a persona on social media. People thought she was shy before then. She was never shy."

Thom cleared his throat. "Earlier you mentioned letters that she received from her readers," he said. "What happened to them?"

"They went to the police." Stephanie Binks stubbed her cigarette out in the grass although she'd taken only a few drags. She turned to face Thom. "Maybe I'll write about a few things that you might be interested in? You'd like to be surprised, wouldn't you?"

When Thom didn't reply, Geneva said, "Do you know why Mira Wallacz was in the woods on the day of her death? Do you have any ideas about that?"

Stephanie Binks smiled, almost shyly. "Mira could be a mystery, couldn't she? I've never understood why she was there. Despite those deplorable bunnies she wrote about for kids, I don't think she even liked—nature."

After the interview Geneva and Thom were silent until they reached the third floor lounge and could be sure they weren't heard.

"My god, I'm still shuddering," Geneva said.

"She likes to insinuate that she knows a lot more than she's willing to tell."

"I suppose she'd be less transparent about her feelings if she did murder Mira," Geneva said. "She disliked her. Even now she can't stand the thought of her. She only agreed to an interview for the attention." She glanced at her phone. No time to wait. They had another interview scheduled: Luisa Chaudette, the fiction writer.

They were passing through the corridor on the fourth floor when they were stopped. The woman introduced herself as Yolanda Eng. "I was Mira's best friend. I heard all about you two. I think I can be useful. Could we talk?"

Geneva remembered her—Yolanda Eng, one of the women by the lake. Geneva had heard her saying she was Mira's oldest friend. "That would be very helpful," Geneva said. "Right now we have an interview scheduled. Tomorrow? Would you be available then?"

No time to think about Yolanda Eng, not when Luisa Chaudette was waiting.

What did Geneva remember about the novelist? She had tried to read one of her novels, but the sex scenes were so deadly—if only they'd been funny or even unintentionally funny. Geneva skimmed the portions about mushroom hunting on the Isle of Mull. In the frequent and disturbingly clinical love scenes, the narrator couldn't stop imagining mushrooms. Which meant the reader couldn't either.

As they approached the writer's room the smell of incense wafted into the hall. Inside, the room was dark. A clothespin held shut a gap between the curtains over the immense window.

In the years since Geneva first saw her, Luisa Chaudette had grown thin. She had changed in other ways too. Her eyebrows rose in permanent surprise, her cheeks puffy, the perfect cheeks of a teenager. Maybe it was valiant when women had work done on their faces. A refusal to bow to time. A floral scarf was loosely wound around Luisa Chaudette's neck, and her skirt was printed with tiny portraits of Frida Kahlo. And still—there was that strange shifting light in her eyes that Geneva remembered. Was she guilty about something? Geneva had wondered as much years ago.

Luisa shook hands with Geneva and Thom, asked them to sit in the two chairs she arranged across from the suite's small dressing table. "I got the impression that the book you're editing won't be overly critical—that you'll include appreciations mostly? I don't think I could write anything academic. Or critical." She flashed a smile at Thom.

"An appreciation would be perfect," he said. "Mira Wallacz's work deserves appreciation."

Luisa Chaudette's eyes were watering when she turned to Geneva. "I'm so glad a collection will be devoted to Mira's work. So far there's just been fluff and sensationalistic stories. The collection you're planning may help keep her name alive too. People will begin forgetting her unless more posthumously published work of hers appears. Her journals, other writing of hers will be discovered, presumably. And that will plump her reputation. Of course the novel that was published last, after her death, reignited a good deal of interest. It was her best work."

"I read in an article that you met her when you were starting out?" Geneva said.

"She was kind to me. I was pretentious and silly and she didn't let me know it. I've changed, I hope. Just as she had changed. I adored her."

Thom must have had long practice listening silently to liars, prevaricators, rationalizers in the confession box. Still, he ought to speak up.

"She changed?" Geneva said, angling her chair closer.

"When her identity was released, that was the big change. As soon as she had an identity to curate she became focused on how people saw her. Her image. No longer the novelist writing under a pseudonym. She wanted to be seen. That may sound desperate, but it's only good business, letting readers identify with you personally. I suppose, for years, I've been tempted to do the same. A career in this publishing climate only lasts for so long. You're considered old goods by the time you're forty. I'm way past that. At least Mira knew how to stay visible. She pulled out all the stops."

She sat back and then forward, rocking, before she said, "You don't have a publisher, do you? I don't think a trade publisher will go for anything you're attempting. I can put you in contact with a small press that might be interested. I could help you figure out a few angles too. That last novel of Mira's, for instance, I gave Mira some tips for that. She was very grateful. Well, I was honored to be of use to her. She always treated me with respect. I appreciated that. Someone does me a kindness and, believe me, I remember."

Geneva couldn't shake the impression that Luisa was enjoying the interview too much. She sounded—triumphant. Like someone who doesn't mind lying when she's sure she can get away with it.

Luisa adjusted her scarf, reknotting the ends. "She defended me. Did you know that? My second book was trounced so much I thought I'd never get another publisher. She vouched for me through her agent. She was still going incognito and didn't have much pull, but she went to bat for me. Then, when her identity was fully revealed people were more interested in her, thanks to her agent. I don't know why she tried to be anonymous for so long. Her sales increased once the cat was out of the bag. Or maybe it was karma—she'd been nice to me so the world was nice to her. Things were always easy for her."

"You still feel that way?" Geneva asked. "That everything was easy for her?"

The Frida Kahlos on Luisa Chaudette's skirt stirred. "I do think it was easy for her. I know that sounds freakish. Those reissued early novels are doing well, even with young adult readers. And her last novel published after her death keeps winning new readers." She looked at Thom, her eyes darkening, and addressed only him. "I should make sure I know what you want."

"We're open to any assessments and any personal reflections," he said. "As long as they're honest."

She smiled more broadly, her gums bright pink. "I could write about the novel published after her death—the last one. From a writer's point of view. That novel will be the one keeping her memory alive. We can all be grateful for that." She brushed at her skirt and two Frida Kahlos winked.

"Are you—a fan of Frida Kahlo?" Geneva asked.

Luisa's smile disappeared. "Not really." She smoothed her skirt. "This was a gift from a reader who thought, mistakenly, that I'm enchanted by human suffering. A misunderstanding."

Maybe it was useless to interview Luisa Chaudette. It's innocent people who feel guilt the most. And for whatever reason, the novelist appeared to feel guilty.

Geneva asked, "Do you know why Mira Wallacz was in the woods on the afternoon she died?"

"I have no idea. None whatsoever. It was such a horrible accident. The ground had to be unsettled. There was a rainstorm earlier in the week. She vanished and turned up there in the woods. So strange. Although Mira was very independent. You never felt you entirely understood what was going on in that head of hers."

In the elevator Thom asked, "Are you hungry?"

"I need to think, Thom. I just need to—"

"You can think while we eat. Tama Squires is up next, right? I've read two of her biographies. We can't deal with her on an empty stomach."

After they ordered at the center's restaurant—cheese fries for both—Geneva said, "Okay. I really have been thinking. About Stephanie Binks, not Luisa Chaudette. Stephanie Binks had a motive. She expected she would inherit everything. Also, Mira's books would be more lucrative if she were dead—that's what Stephanie Binks suggested. I don't know if that can be right, but maybe it could be right in the mind of an agent. What bothered me most was her claim that Mira wanted to kill herself. Do you think that's true?"

"No, that's not true."

"And you're sure."

"I'm sure," he said. "Nothing could be more unlikely. What about Luisa Chaudette?"

"The jealousy she felt toward Mira Wallacz—that's evident. She certainly wanted us to know we won't get a trade publisher. There's something odd about her, like she wouldn't participate in violence but might passively enjoy someone else's violence. I tried to read one of her books. She's a voyeuristic sort of person, if her writing is any indication of her personality."

Thom Crystl grinned. "What have you gotten me into?"

Geneva paused before she said, "It's becoming real, isn't it? We could get an edited collection of essays published. You could soothe your conscience. I mean, your conscience about what we're doing—these interviews. We really can get essays from these people or some kind of reflections and actually see about publishing them. What we're doing, it can manifest as a reality, right? You don't have to feel guilty."

"Guilt isn't always a negative," he said.

"All right," she agreed. "I know you're going to say guilt can guide behavior. Because you have a very active conscience. You must have. But what we're doing—it's not wrong. It's in pursuit of truth."

"I'm not sure there's a truth to be discovered, Geneva."

She felt her throat close and managed to say, "That would be such a shame, Thom."

⧈ Chapter Thirteen

Tama Squires emailed that they should meet her in the seventh-floor lounge, "past the last restroom, take a right. Looks like you're hitting a wall. Take a left."

The biographer's orange sleeves were printed with gray check marks and dropped down over her fingers after she released Thom's hand.

A white couch that nestled against the wall was overwhelmed with a dark and furry covering that looked like buffalo hide. A coffee table squeezed between a chair and another smaller furless sofa. To Geneva's right a bank of windows looked out to a rim of the lake and farther into the tree line. What could be seen from such a height ten years ago?

Tama Squires was already speaking before Geneva and Thom settled on the couch facing her. "I bet you're full of questions, you two. I can see it in your faces. Let's have at it." Geneva had never been close enough to notice the mole on Tama's lip—it moved, not unattractively. Her caftan billowed around her while she squirmed to get more comfortable.

Geneva decided that being direct with Tama Squires was their best course. "Do you mind if I take notes?" she asked. "We'll be writing an introduction to the collection, and of course we'll have to draw from your biography—fully acknowledged—and we're wondering if there could be more you might want to tell us about the circumstances ten years ago. Since that time, any further thoughts? You were here, after all, when the tragedy happened."

Tama Squires barked out a laugh. "You are a couple of ghouls, aren't you? Although I suppose it's necessary to put things in context. You could record me, if that would help? But I guess note-taking is still—useful." She sat forward and patted Geneva's knee. "You look like the sort of person who takes good notes. Go ahead. You never learned to trust your memory, no doubt. Who among us does?"

Geneva put down her pen.

"I knew immediately when I got the email what you're really interested in," Tama Squires said. "The whole drama of Mira's death. That's what you want to write about. Don't pretend otherwise. If Mira hadn't died I would never have sold my last manuscript or sold it only to a university press—that's what I thought back then. Her reputation is even stronger now that she's been dead a decade. I suppose I might have gone with a better publisher after all."

She was focused on Geneva so fully that Thom seemed to disappear into shadow. The biographer patted Geneva's knee again. "I recognize you," she said. "That's how I know what you're up to."

Geneva's face heated. "You recognize me?"

Tama laughed, proud of herself and not disguising it. "You're not quite the same, surely. You had to change over time. We all do. You somehow trained the victimhood out of yourself. I guess you had to grow up a bit. There was a while when I thought, because you were with Mira out there in the sticks, that you were the culprit and attacked Mira. Or that something about you attracted violence. You looked so young and lost, an easy target. You resemble Mira, you know that? In certain lights. You look more like her now than you did back then."

"I don't think so," Geneva said. Thom had said the same thing. Maybe it was inevitable. Read enough of an author and you become like the author in one dimension or more? Or maybe Geneva's wardrobe derived from Mira's books—all those women in white blouses and slim skirts and cardigans. Did she think like Mira too? Sometimes Geneva couldn't stop imagining people's inner thoughts. That was something she learned, in part, from reading Mira's books. But what could she do? She couldn't stop thinking. Or reading.

Tama was still speaking. "I thought the police were letting you go out of some bizarre idea that females aren't violence-prone. You were so strange, floating about. A number of us noticed. And then you saw Mira in among all those trees and didn't tell us. You had talked to her too. You came galloping back to the conference center and just stood around waiting with the rest of us like the cat who swallowed the canary."

Geneva drew her shoulders back. "Mira didn't want me to announce—"

"So she wanted to make an entrance? I believe that. Also—she would have enjoyed keeping us waiting. I predicted that too."

Geneva was quick to defend Mira Wallacz and herself. "She said she wanted to walk back to the conference center by herself and that she had something she needed to do. It was disclosed that she'd been looking at some properties earlier. So when I was with her she was on her way back to the conference. I assumed she'd be returning. I thought maybe she just wanted time there among those trees. For some reason or other. Maybe you know the reason why she didn't return right away?"

A look of satisfaction crossed Tama Squires's face. "It wasn't random, her being where she was. She had a reason."

"How do you know?" Thom asked. Geneva felt a blast of gratitude toward him. He shook his head before he went on. "It's not in your biography."

Tama lifted her arms, the fabric of her caftan's sleeves sliding to her elbows. She rested her hands in her lap. For a moment she looked weirdly docile. "A little confession," she said, her laugh revealing very white teeth. "I would have known why she was tromping around in the bushes if I had read all the letters in my possession. You know how it is. There was far, far too much material to go through while I was writing the biography. And I had a deadline. What was I to do? Given the time constraints. You can't imagine how many letters there were. Mira was basically a graphomaniac. She lived with her own mother at the very end, god help us, but anytime she was away from her there were letters between them, almost all from Mira. How could anyone read all that miserable stuff? Plus, my publisher wanted the biography to come out while Mira's death and the strange circumstances surrounding it were still on people's minds."

She turned away from Geneva to focus on Thom. "Maybe you know about this sort of thing," she said to him. "You're a writer, after all. There's always a problem once a book is published. Some hole or gap or even a knot where things don't make sense. We all know there had to be a reason for Mira to be doing whatever she did, possibly a reason that was private. I went back to some xeroxes of correspondence and started skimming."

She patted her own knees and sighed. "For your essay collection I could look back at my experience writing the bio—my professional and personal experience might make an interesting piece. How does that sound if I write it up?"

"But why was she in the woods?" Geneva asked, unable to keep impatience out of her voice.

Tama sucked in her lower lip.

Geneva wondered, could the biographer be any more annoying if she tried?

"Oh, that's something I'm keeping quiet for a while," Tama said. "I might answer that question in writing, not in conversation." She sighed again, more heavily. "Have you considered that a disaffected reader might be the murderer? She got some awful letters. Her agent showed me some. You met her—Mira's agent? Stephanie Binks. She's here at the conference." Tama laughed. "You'll get a kick out of this, but if you ever put it in your book I'll sue you for more than you're worth. Years ago I played a little trick on Mira. I actually threatened to sue her. Your face, Thom—like you've never been sued. I told Mira that a character, the biographer in her fourth novel, was based on me and that she had to give me a percentage or I'd take her to court. I was only half-kidding, although I have to tell you I come from a family of full-on jokers. My brother used to clerk in a drugstore and stick pins in half the condoms. A lot of kids in Havre de Grace owe their existence to him. Anyway, one of Mira's characters was a biographer with a name similar to mine and with my own hobbies—she liked to can pickles. She was accused of killing her great aunt. Not that I was accused of killing anyone in my family."

"I remember that novel," Geneva said. "You actually think she modeled the character after you? Or was it all just a bad joke? And the character didn't can pickles she canned peaches."

"I don't think so. I have a very good memory for pickles. The thing is, I just wanted to have a genuine conversation with Mira. I thought threatening to sue her was a possible avenue for beginning a conversation."

"Did it work?" Thom asked.

"No. She had me talk to Stephanie Binks. Do you know that Mira was shopping around for another agent within weeks of her death? She was keeping it quiet, making, you know—inquiries. She could have anyone as an agent, but she had particular requirements. Honesty and a lack of curiosity, that's my best guess."

"Did Stephanie Binks know she was going to be dropped?"

"I imagine so. Word spreads. But people wouldn't want to offend Stephanie and be the messenger of bad news. She has such a temper—it's legendary. She must have taken it hard when she found out she wasn't anywhere in the will and wasn't getting another cent from poor Mira. Not that Mira was poor. Maybe she was a little self-destructive, as artists generally are."

Recalling the interview with Stephanie Binks and the agent's grotesque assertion, Geneva asked, "Do you think Mira Wallacz predicted her own death?"

"Of course not—despite Mira's final novel. That would be awful, wouldn't it—if what we wrote condemned us to the same fate as our characters? There wouldn't be a mystery novelist alive on the planet. Not to mention the thriller writers. So many writers are ghouls, writing about what they fear and then acting it all out on characters who usually turn out to be amalgams of their mothers, neighbors, and childhood friends. At least the lives I write about are ready-made. I don't have to imagine the worst for my subjects now that I'm only writing about the newly dead. They've already lived their fates. When it comes to what happened to Mira, I know that murder is juicier to contemplate, yet there's a part of me that believes an accidental death fit her plots better than murder. All those coincidences, the way cause and effect never quite matched. The world in her novels was just one accidental coincidence after another waiting to happen. Sorry to sound cynical, but I don't think our thirst for meaning can be slaked by the indifference of the universe."

Geneva was sure Tama Squires had made this same speech before. It sounded memorized. She couldn't hold back her questions any longer. "When Mira Wallacz died—were you here, in this lounge? Could you see anything from this height?"

Tama stood and walked to the window. "What could anyone see from here?" She craned her neck, peering across the grounds toward the lake and the tree line. "I don't recall where I was when it must have happened."

Thom turned to Geneva. "What do you think she could possibly see?" He sounded suspicious, or teasing, or irritated. As if he wasn't on her side.

Tama backed away from the window and sat down again, groaning as she lowered herself. "You're not really even editing a collection, are you? You keep giving yourselves away." She chuckled and rubbed her own cheek. "Don't worry. Your secret is safe with me. I'd check out Inger Delft if I were you. She was on the program back then with a title like 'The Future Mira Wallacz.' Wow—did she ever miss out. It was supposed to be a takedown. Who does that? Other than an enemy? I was looking forward to that whole scene."

"Do you think Inger Delft will be willing to talk to us?" Geneva asked. "I didn't know she was going to be here this year. I didn't email her."

"Are you kidding? She'll be chomping at the bit. Anything to ruin a reputation, even though poor Mira can't defend herself from the grave. Also, check out Luisa Chaudette, if you haven't arranged to interview her already. I don't know if Mira recognized how much Luisa didn't like her. Despised her really. Mira gave Luisa a beautiful blurb and what does Luisa do? She goes on Goodreads under multiple aliases and gives Mira terrible reviews for every single one of her books. Is that a friend? I don't think so. Luisa was jealous ever since an idiot had a line from one of Mira's books tattooed on his backside. Some undertaker is going to enjoy seeing that. A tattoo is nothing to be jealous of, but leave it to Luisa to envy even the dead."

Thom's smile was frozen.

Tama continued. "In some ways that biography of Mira never lets me go. I'm thinking of writing something that looks closer at her death. Maybe I could write a piece that's short and provocative for your collection. Double dip to get interest going."

Thom pulled at his shirt sleeve and didn't look up when he spoke. "What sort of angle will you pursue?"

"I suppose I can give you a taste to whet your appetite. I'm thinking of calling the book *The Afterlife of an Author*. I'll look at the posthumously published work that's coming out. Also there's a good deal to say about how Mira influenced other writers, and about the reception of her work. Trying to figure out the magic. I'm not sure I understand that magic myself, even though Mira and I had so much in common. I'm a storyteller too. Except my stories aren't invented. They're born from reality and shaped. Do I sound like I'm reciting a lecture? Possibly I am. I really need to use some of what I just said to you for my talk tomorrow. You're coming, aren't you?" She was only looking at Thom, as if his attendance was what mattered.

Geneva said, "You don't think you've already examined enough about the end of Mira's life in the biography?"

Tama gave a laugh that resembled a cough. "There's so much more I could say. I ignored a few things in my rush to write the biography, as I told you. I always say, the secret to success is learning what to ignore. But it's possible to ignore too much." She smiled at Geneva. "Remember my words. The past is never past. Faulkner supposedly said those words, but I said them for years before I knew he said them."

Geneva stood. "Thanks for everything. We'll be in touch."

"It's been a pleasure," the biographer said. "I think I'll just stay up here a while. I like my privacy. Come to my talk tomorrow. I'll make it interesting." She gave a tiny, non-convincing, self-deprecating chuckle before she said, "I knew when I got your email that you're opening up the question of Mira's death and her possible murder. I knew that instantly, even if you're now trying to cover it up. Sensationalizing her death. Creating a little spin-off about it. Good for you. You'll never secure a publisher otherwise. All I can say is, remember: most murders are unsolved, and the waffling inept coroner here in Bingle never inspired confidence. I guess the moral is: don't stand underneath a slope littered with loose rocks if you don't want your murderer to get away with it." She smiled before she said, "Good luck. There may be a podcast in this, I suppose. For someone. I'd take a stab at it, but a podcast's not my cup of tea. Not yet anyway."

The scent of perfume, lilac. A woman, her long black hair in tight braids, was in the lounge. "Ah, Lizette," Tama cried out, "meet Geneva and Thom, they're pumping me for information about what happened ten years ago. I feel like an old-school historian."

Tama introduced Lizette as her wife. It was clear that she couldn't wait anymore for Geneva and Thom to leave. She stood from the couch, pointed at Geneva, and said, "What's that?"

The ink from Geneva's pen had bled across her notebook. The inky strings, together, looked so much like a stand of trees that the shapes hardly seemed accidental.

Once they were in the hotel's first floor lobby Geneva questioned Thom.

"When I asked Tama Squires about the view from the lounge why did you cut me off?"

He stopped walking and turned to her. "You went too far. The look on your face, your tone of voice—you were insinuating that she saw something. That maybe she could be protecting someone. You sounded ready to call her a liar. She'd never talk to us again if you kept it up."

Geneva ducked her head and lowered her voice. "She is a liar. She misdirects people. She clutches her secrets to her chest in that big caftan of hers. That's the sin of omission, right? You must be an authority on sins."

He let her words pass. "No one likes to be pressured," he said. "You were leading her to remember. Her memory could be distorted, falsified, if you aren't careful with her. Besides, if she saw anything she would have reported it. Or if she suddenly remembered something it should come spontaneously. Don't lead her. Some people, they're led easily."

"She doesn't seem easily led. She seems stubborn."

"That's because she has to protect herself. All I mean is: your tone was a little too forceful."

"It was?"

"It doesn't take all that much to screw up a person's thought processes."

"How do you know this? False confessions in the confession box?"

"You could say that."

She paused to consider how her own tone of voice was affecting him before she said, "I'm sorry. I really am. I guess I need a drink. How about you?"

"Drinking—it's not something I can do and still remain . . ."

"What?"

"I was going to say sane but I meant sober. It's hard to stop once I start. My mind isn't under my control—at all—if I drink. Let's get out of here. Those cheese fries, they didn't do it for us, I'm pretty sure."

He drove them to a restaurant in Bingle's town center. Glass crystals were suspended in tiers from branching ceiling fixtures. In the painting above their table the scene resembled the lake near the conference center, lines of oaks and pines circling the horizon.

They were the only customers. A young waitress, hair in a top-knot and wearing a black sweater spattered with silver sparkles, looked glad to see them.

Geneva realized she had been clenching her fists. Biting her lip too. Soon the wine was relaxing her—and something was relaxing Thom, although he had made do with a non-alcoholic spritzer. They both ordered the scallops.

"Mine are wonderful. They—melt."

He smiled, agreeing. The scallops were buttery, soaked in cream with smashed cherries. Nestled in the cream sauce beside the scallops: an island of whipped potatoes.

"It doesn't get a whole lot better than this," he said. "You're happy? I can tell you are."

She liked that, liked that he cared how she felt, liked that her contentment appeared to intensify his own.

They reviewed the day's interviews. Each person they had talked to so far had a motive. The agent Stephanie Binks mistakenly believed she stood to gain from Mira's death, as the will's executor and beneficiary. In turn, Mira's books would gain readers from a sensational murder or unexplained accident, and Stephanie Binks, who must have known about the unpublished novel, would be in a position to negotiate for more from publishers, including more international rights. And Luisa Chaudette? She defended Mira yet even now appeared to envy her. Maybe for certain people a rival's death can't quell their competitive instincts. The mix of envy and resentment and pretend-affection she displayed was suspicious. Could it lead to a person picking up a stone and giving it a good throw at someone's head? As for the biographer, Tama Squires, she was so self-dramatizing she might have wanted to keep extending drama outward to make her biography more saleable with Mira's death or even with Mira having suffered an accident. If she had been willing to tell a fake story to Mira—that she was going to sue her—what other deceptions was she capable of?

For Geneva the experience of interviewing the women was like being at work again, among puffy egoists and their secret dilemmas, the hardened faces that could dissolve in a moment and reveal an unendurable vulnerability. Many times she had wanted to flee into a back room, close the door, and never again listen to aggrieved clients. Aida, more indifferent to appeals, was far better suited for the job. What Geneva didn't mention to Thom: here at the conference, combined with the sort of squeamish lack of authority she suffered as an imposter, she endured a creeping sense that things could go terribly wrong. Is this how people lose their minds?

For ten years the death of Mira Wallacz had stalked her thoughts. Yet at least now she was trying to tease meaning from shadows—even if finding out what actually happened might be impossible.

She set down her empty wine glass. "Every time we talked to those people I kept thinking: That's it, there's the killer. Then, minutes later, I thought: no, that's not a murderer. I've been feeling utterly confused when I'm not feeling angry. Everyone had such mixed feelings for Mira Wallacz. Nevertheless, she might actually have thought they supported her or—I don't know. Maybe it really is like Agatha Christie's *Murder on the Orient Express* and everyone we've talked to wanted to kill her. Or else they're here to kill someone else? I'm still haunted by Stephanie Binks's claim that Mira wanted to die."

Thom blinked. "Mira wanted to live. Maybe she just didn't want to live in the same way she had been living."

"What makes you think that?"

"I'm speculating. Have to stop that. That way danger lies."

"We're in danger then. Maybe there weren't a lot of people Mira could count on in the end. But you—I've wondered: did she think she owed you a debt? Was that why she left you everything?"

He wiped at the table with his napkin. "She owed me nothing. I owed her—for being good to us. It was difficult when my brother and I were kids. My folks were always having trouble. Mira must have heard the fighting between our parents. She lived right next door when she was still with her mother. She never made us feel embarrassed, no matter how much she heard. She thought I was destined to be a writer even when I was a kid. I'd show her my silly little poems and she'd praise them to the skies. So when I left for seminary she was concerned. She believed I'd chosen the wrong vocation. Look." He opened his wallet and unfolded a piece of paper. "She wrote my name and put gold stars all around the edges of this certificate she created, my official certificate as a writer she called it. I was eleven years old when she gave me this. I've kept it ever since. I knew I wanted a life that was separate from the life I'd known at home—and the priesthood seemed like a good bet for that. My father's uncle was a priest. It was a serious thing to do on my father's side of the family. A genuine choice. My father was proud of my brother George and how he wanted, since he was a kid, to join the priesthood. Maybe my father would have been proud of both of us. It was hard after he died. At least George and I had each other for a few years. And then George left for seminary and my mother and I were alone. It didn't take long before I felt called. I wasn't, not really. I mistook a general restlessness for what my brother felt. I believed I was saving myself, not only my soul. My mother wasn't happy but dealt with it. She went into counseling after I left home and of course Mira's mother—Eileen—helped her. They were very close, my mother and Eileen. I wasn't much help. I still don't know if I deserve to be forgiven."

"You were a priest. You have to believe in forgiveness."

"Maybe that's why I'm no longer a priest."

Geneva pushed her plate away. "So it wasn't just a case of Mira giving you and your brother cookies. She cared a great deal about you both. Is he like you, your brother?"

The waitress stopped and refilled their water glasses. After she left Thom said, "George's parish is in San Diego. He works with a population that has dealt with trauma. He's changing lives, making a big difference. He knew he wanted to be a priest even when we were just little kids. When I was seventeen I was following in his footsteps, not really thinking for myself. Mira and Mira's mother and mine, they all resisted the idea. And then in seminary and afterward the thought of writing was too much on my mind, distracting me from my obligations. I admired my brother and his choice. I wanted to help people, to give people comfort. It didn't occur to me that if I couldn't even comfort myself, what did I think I was doing? I suppose Mira imagined that willing me her money would give me time to write eventually. That's the only reason I can think of for why my name was in her will. Taking the money never seemed right to me. I'd cheated the Church. I came in as a fake, really."

"Didn't you want to give the money to your mother?"

"I wanted to give some to my mother—Mira would have liked that. My mother wouldn't take it. It came from death, she said. She said it wouldn't be right. I don't regret my choice. The parish uses the money for the pantry, for social programs, for upkeep of the church. There are plenty of needs in that church that the inheritance can be used for. My mother approved of my giving the money away. I think she felt rejuvenated after I left the priesthood. The last time I saw her she looked years younger. She put on weight, thank god, and started caring about her health. She'll want to hear about this conference. She was always interested in Mira."

"Were Mira and your mother close?"

"My mother was close to Mira's mother. Eileen—that was Mira's mother—was respected in town. She ran the strawberry festival and the cat rescue. Maybe that's why Mira kept her identity secret as a novelist for so long. To protect Eileen. None of us knew Mira wrote the novels—our Mira. The kiddie books, that was okay, that was acceptable. But the novels, no. People were upset when they found out. They kept recognizing themselves in her characters. Even my mother thought she was represented. I could never figure out which character she thought was her."

"How did your mother deal with that?"

"Fuming. She was protective of Eileen, and so she managed to get used to what Eileen's daughter had done. My mother's pretty self-sufficient. Tough. She lives outside Newark. I'll see her in a month or so."

"She must be incredibly proud of you for your poetry."

He blushed and once again looked younger.

"Being a poet—that strikes her as not a lot better than being a priest. She's busy on Facebook and Instagram—not posting so much as following a lot of people. She was struck hard by Eileen's death. But she's better now—taking exercise classes, making friends."

"She's not Catholic?"

"Oh no. She says any established religion is only a cult with power. George hates hearing that, but he's learned to laugh it off. Maybe, by now, she's secretly proud of the choice he made. My being a poet—not so much. I'm pretty sure she finds it embarrassing."

Images were coming for Geneva that had nothing to do with Mira Wallacz: she remembered slipping to the floor at the party, Thom's arm wrapped around her, their faces close, laughing. And then driving him to his hotel, her window rolled down because she wanted the air on her face, the near sting of it. And the next day— the regret, her heart sinking. She should have followed him into his hotel or brought him to her apartment.

She asked, "Do you know that when we first met I had the wild impression that you wanted me to confess?"

He laughed, tossing his head back.

"Never. The last thing I wanted, believe me."

"But you did give that impression."

"You've done nothing wrong."

He took the check when it came.

"I can't let you," she said, although her bank balance was the lowest it had been in a year.

"I have an inheritance," he said.

"But you gave it away."

"I couldn't give all of it away. That's part of the trouble. I have to pay a lawyer to do my thinking for me. I keep stocks so they'll grow. It's up to the lawyer. He has to be paid. The money has to be managed. I don't want it for myself. But it's not so easy to get rid of. And if the money can grow, that will help to make sure there's more available to help the congregation—and others. Don't ask me to explain all this. I can't."

The meal is on Mira Wallacz then, Geneva thought.

They were back in Thom's car when she said, "You've never told me so much about your life until today." She didn't say what she was thinking: he must be beginning to trust her.

"I thought maybe you should know more." He hesitated and then said, "I don't think you need me for anything now. You're doing most of the interviewing. I sit there, hardly knowing what to say. I really think you might be more effective on your own."

"You're not interested in continuing?" she asked.

He was driving more slowly, concentrating on his words. "I understand that you believed you needed me to give credibility to your plans because I'm recognized in a few quarters as a writer. Now I'm really not needed. You're an excellent interviewer. You're gifted at getting these people to talk. You give them your full attention. You never needed me in the first place. If you have to do this detective work that you're attempting—I don't think you have to—you can do this without anyone's help."

When she didn't respond he went on. "Geneva, I know you think what we're doing is necessary. I know you think you need to do this to gain peace for yourself. I wanted to help you, and I've tried to imagine how you're dealing with all this, how the memory of what happened to Mira has preyed on you. I'm not useful to you. I'm not helping. If anything it seems to me that it's all the more clear that—"

She didn't wait to hear more. "You've been humoring me," she said. "You don't suspect anyone. Even though any one of these people could have harmed Mira. They resented her."

"It's not the same as wanting to destroy someone," he said, his voice strained. "What they want, it's adulation. And a sense that they're recognized, not unknown. They want more meaning in their lives. Don't judge them."

She stroked the back of her neck where the muscles were suddenly tight. Maybe she was judging everyone. How could she find out the truth otherwise? What was wrong with judging anyone? It was her human right. You can't protect yourself if you don't exercise judgment. Maybe Thom Crystl had been in a cloistered environment for too long. He didn't suspect anyone of wrongdoing, except maybe himself. He didn't really understand that Mira Wallacz hadn't been given justice, that there were still questions about her death. Maybe he understood on a logical level, not emotionally.

She asked, trying to keep her voice light, teasing, "You say that these people want adulation. You don't want adulation?"

"It would terrify me. Listen, I don't think I should continue with what we've been doing. I apologize, Geneva. I can't pretend otherwise. The sin of omission would be not to tell you. Listen. Really listen and think. You heard some people talking ten years ago and you tried to fill in what you heard to force Mira's death to make sense in the way her novels make sense. I'm sure more than ever that what happened was an accident. An uncanny accident. There's no real motive strong enough for any of these women. Stephanie Binks as Mira's agent would lose her greatest asset, her largest source of income. I have no idea what it would mean to have an agent, but I can't believe Stephanie Binks would harm the person who guarantees her an immense income—a continuing source. Any posthumous publications would dry up eventually. It would make no sense for her to harm Mira. She seems truthful too, too candid. Ready to admit her own resentments."

Thom's driving had speeded up by the time Geneva said, "I don't know anything about agents, but I've lived enough to know enough not to trust people who have something to sell. What about Luisa Chaudette? She didn't raise any red flags?"

Thom pulled into the parking lot at the conference center and parked. He turned to Geneva. "Luisa Chaudette seems like a helpless sort of person, too self-involved to actually harm anyone else. And Tama Squires—she could have had an opportunity for yet another book about Mira's continued life. The longer Mira lived the more she'd have to write about."

"I'm not sure that's true about Tama Squires. Mira Wallace's death was an open mystery. And an open mystery is good for sales."

He unbuckled his seat belt. "It's been an experiment—what we've been doing. Gathering information. You have to realize it's going nowhere and my being part of the process—it's not fair to you. It's not right. You have more reason to suspect me than any of the people you've interviewed. I feel more guilty than any of them. You were here the first time when you were still an idealistic kid. You're still—somewhat like that. You're judging these women as you did then, without tolerance for the fact that they're not perfect, that they didn't worship at the same altar as you did. You want there to be a reason behind Mira's death—you want someone to be punished. You want to be the instrument of justice. I don't mean to hurt your feelings. Forgive me, Geneva. I have to be honest with you."

She could have argued, but then she'd respect herself less.

He held the elevator as she stepped out to head to her room. A door opened in the hallway and slammed shut just as quickly. Thom flinched at the sound. He was nervous, Geneva thought, because he'd told her the truth. He told her that he wasn't needed, but what he meant was that she wasn't needed, not by him. He confided in her so that he could leave, innocent and free.

⊁ Chapter Fourteen

BETWEEN THE PARTED CURTAINS the sky was a deepening slate. The walkway was empty except for a skinny man taking a cigarette break. On Monday Geneva could refuse to explain herself to Aida. She could say she tried and failed and expected nothing more. She always expected too much or not enough. The balance was never correct.

A blast of shame. Thom was right to leave. She had forced him into her scheme, relied on his pity, his guilt, his agreeable, unself-forgiving nature. And there was a lie hovering—her own lie, the lie that she was only seeking justice for Mira Wallacz. She needed to admit it to herself: she was dealing with infatuation, the sparks and shadows of her feelings for Thom Crystl. Which meant she was, in some part of herself, using a much-loved writer's death for her own small, selfish purpose.

And yet. And yet. To stop from drowning in self-disgust, she told herself something else that was also true. That October after-noon in the woods a decade ago she had encountered evil. The in-tuition was as real as a thorn snagging her skin. And now she could not dispel her belief that she should have kept hold of Mira Wal-lacz's hand and never left her. And, yes, Thom Crystl had been more than the object of infatuation. She recited to herself her fa-miliar reasons: his reputation had made it possible to secure interviews with more seasoned participants at the conference. And she had needed him because he knew Mira Wallacz since boyhood and would observe what she might not. Then too, the fact that Thom Crystl had come into her life at a party—that was more than a sign, even more than an invitation. It was a summons. If she hadn't met him she wouldn't have searched online for his identity and found his connection to Mira—and discovered information about the conference honoring Mira Wallacz's legacy. Maybe her attraction to Thom was never accidental. Maybe some force in the world wanted truth to be discovered for Mira Wallacz, a writer who unraveled her plots to arrive at justice, unmistakable justice. And now Geneva herself was an instrument of justice. Or maybe it was arrogant to think that way?

She was about to close the curtains when she saw a figure, gait halting, crossing the parking lot. Tama Squires was approaching the conference center's east entrance.

Geneva pulled on a sweater and raced out of her room. She should be able to catch Tama if the elevator would ever arrive. In the lobby she spun around, wondering if the biographer had yet made it past the lobby. She felt a hand on her shoulder and turned to see Tama grinning.

"I was looking for you," Geneva said.

"I know," Tama gasped. "People so often are."

Two clerks were texting behind the reception desk. Geneva and Tama settled on armchairs near the artificial fireplace.

"I have a question," Geneva said.

"First," Tama said, "let me catch my breath." The biographer slumped in her chair. At last she said. "I was just out for a walk. It helps my nerves. Lets me calm down when I get claustrophobic. Now what do you want from me?"

"I can't stop thinking about what you said earlier—that Mira had a reason for being in the woods, and that you know what it is."

"You haven't guessed?"

"I hate guessing. I can promise you your theory will never be published by me or by Thom. I just need to know what your theory is."

A crowd was coming through the entrance. Tama sank lower, scooted her chair closer to a pillar. When the lobby quieted, Tama asked, "Why is it so important to you?"

"You're right. It is important to me." Geneva had to stop herself from grasping Tama's hand. "Do you think I haven't terrorized myself for years with memories of that afternoon? I need to know all I can. You know I was there. No one else here does—other than Thom."

Tama craned to look behind her. When she turned back she lowered her voice. "Listen, it shouldn't be such a mystery why Mira was where she was. I probably didn't even require any letter to make it all come clear. Common sense might have helped me out." Her eyes were nearly closed. A tremble passed over her face. "As I told you and your friend Thom, there were too many letters to read. I finally got around to a letter from Mira's mother describing her favorite place. So that was where Mira must have gone—to her mother's favorite place. For her own special reason."

"What reason? I don't understand."

"It's simple. But really, why should I tell you? You're a competitor. I'm saving what I know for my own work." She paused and smiled. "You look like you're ready to slap me. I wouldn't try that if I were you. Watch your temper, Geneva."

The rain continued through the night, sizzling against the window of Geneva's room. She woke from a blast of thunder. The next morning beer-colored foam floated along the lake's rim.

Geneva's anger was rooting deeper. Anger at hideous Tama Squires for baiting her with that story about knowing what Mira Wallacz was doing in the woods on the last day of her life. Tama probably didn't even know—could only speculate. She dangled her speculation over Geneva's head, like the mean sadist she was. And Thom—of course he didn't have to come with her. He shouldn't have, given how he so easily stepped away from helping her. Pity—it had been about pity, his agreement to accompany her. Thank god he quit the priesthood. He could have demoralized an entire congregation. He was weak enough that he'd gone along with her only to please her, hadn't the strength to refuse. If she felt disappointed and saddened last night, today she endured the hot bubbling of anger.

⊁ CHAPTER FIFTEEN

O VER THE COLD MUFFINS, tepid coffee, clear glass canisters of boiled eggs, the horrible-smelling sausage, the first rumors began. Tama's wife Lizette hurried up and leaned close to Geneva. "You saw her when she came back in from walking last night. She told me. Have you seen her since then? She went out again. We had a disagreement. I told her not to go—and now—I can't find her."

When Geneva answered, Lizette frowned and skittered off to another table. Geneva followed and asked if there might be a note somewhere, if Tama was answering her phone. "She's always forgetting to charge it," Lizette said.

Geneva pictured the biographer stalking the grounds in her enormous caftan, then losing energy, collapsing. "You talked to the organizers?" Geneva asked. "To the hotel staff?"

"They're looking around the property. I didn't want to get in their way."

Several women were crowding around Lizette. One broke off from the others. "We'll help," Yolanda Eng announced. "You remember me?" she asked Geneva before taking her arm and volunteering them both.

The two women took the path by the lake. Mist still hadn't cleared. The day was overcast and reeds near the water's edge hardly swayed.

"Tama thinks she's invincible and can plow around in the dark all night," Yolanda told Geneva. "Though there's always the possibility she was seeing someone else and spending the night in another room. You notice how she enjoys Luisa Chaudette's company? I don't think Lizette even notices how often she's with Luisa."

"She could be hurt," Geneva said. "We can't waste time."

Soon they were both nearly jogging, scattering leaves. They slowed their pace to catch their breath. Breathing heavily, Yolanda said, "Wouldn't it be outrageous if what happened to Mira happened to Tama?"

"Maybe she got lost," Geneva said. "The woods are thick back here, with all sorts of hillocks."

"Hillocks," Yolanda said. "I grew up here, but you talk about the woods as if you know them better than I do. Maybe you do. What was Tama wearing yesterday? It might help us to spot her."

"A caftan. Orange."

Yolanda looked up. "Be careful of loose rocks," she said. "Whenever we're under a slope we're vulnerable to rolling projectiles." Her voice betrayed excitement, not fear. She laughed before she went on, "If Tama got this far she really did want to escape civilization. Or else she was targeted."

Who would target Tama? Without a doubt, the biographer could be annoying. Her self-certainty inflated into profound self-importance. In some ways that tendency might become endearing. What would it be like, Geneva wondered, to exist without self-doubt, without backtracking on your own instincts?

Yolanda was breathing so hard that Geneva slowed her pace again.

A flutter of coppery color.

Yolanda gasped. "Oh crud, it's a log. Tama would be furious if she knew I mistook a log for her. I really hope no one attacked her."

The lake made soft shirring noises and a comical gulp. Yolanda went on. "Being here among the rocks and trees and the what-do-you-call-them—hillocks?—and the ground sloping toward the lake—it's hard not to think about Mira. Every night I keep hoping I'll dream about her, that she'll come to me in a dream and comfort me. You know what else I keep thinking about? *The Wizard of Oz.* How in the movie the trees throw apples at Dorothy. Enraged trees. Nature rebelling. Mira was really lucky she wasn't hit by a boulder, though I suppose the end result would be the same. Boulders, left by the glaciers. Millenia ago." She sighed before asking, "Do you ever worry about sinkholes? Limestone. You could disappear and no one would know. You'd be sucked down, and unless someone noticed and gave a damn you'd be lost forever."

When Yolanda began to walk off the path Geneva steered her back. "You know," Yolanda said, "Mira Wallacz was a bit of a mystic or, at any rate, she appreciated the mystic in me. When you get around to interviewing me for your little book I can go into that in depth. She encouraged that part of me. It's in the novels, all those subtle supernatural grace notes. Those are from me. People think she was mainly writing realistic novels with a romantic tinge or trace, but the mysteries in those novels kept regenerating. I used to tell her that it was like starfish—how the arms grow back, how every novel of hers kept retrieving something from another world, a world of the spirit, the one world we can only intuit, not entirely imagine. You know I have nightmares about how she died? For stones to hit her head from a height around here, maybe she was sitting on the ground or kneeling? I mean the cliffs are treacherous on this side of the lake and the rocks can slide, true. She was struck near one of the east side slopes, that's what the newspaper accounts reported. It was a terrible fate, wasn't it? Like St. Stephen.

The first martyr stoned to death. Just thinking about Mira always makes me sad. God, I loved her. Loved her so much."

They were circling back toward the south patio when shouts erupted.

An ambulance, idling, had pulled close to the center's entrance. In the crowd that gathered Geneva recognized Lizette first.

"The branch was dead," an obviously proud paramedic told the group while his coworkers hoisted the stretcher. "She must have run into the branch. Cracked it right off. It was hanging low. If it hadn't been decaying—"

He didn't finish the thought. Yolanda, at Geneva's side, whispered, "So her head is harder than wood."

Someone murmured, "Poor dear. She's going to be wearing a hat for the rest of her life."

As the ambulance pulled away, Stephanie Binks came forward and put an arm around Lizette. "I'll take you to the hospital in my car. No worries. She'll be all right." The words were spoken with such concern and sympathy that Geneva felt a draft of guilt for her suspicions about the agent.

Already the widespread atmosphere at the conference had moved into a tittery tone of delight and expectation, enlivening everyone. Geneva knew because she felt it herself.

Beside Geneva, Yolanda was whispering. "Rocks. Trees. Nature's in revolt. Punishing the truth tellers."

Hearing Yolanda was more aggravating than Geneva could bear.

She wished Thom was among the group and wondered where he was, if he already checked out of the conference hotel. She couldn't help thinking of the coincidences—two head wounds in the woods near the center: Mira's fatal, Tama's perhaps nearly fatal. It was almost artful, the terrible symmetry.

⸙ CHAPTER SIXTEEN

AFTER THE EXCITEMENT surrounding Tama's accident had dissipated, Geneva settled at a table on the conference center's west patio, about to gather her thoughts, when she was interrupted.

"I heard about your essay collection. Are you free for coffee? I think I can help. I'm Inger. Inger Delft." The woman's eyes were a pale blue, like those of certain sled dogs. Her hair was coming undone from two long gray and wheat-colored braids.

Geneva followed the woman to the conference center's barroom and cafe, windowless and dimly lit. Neither looked at the coffee menu. Inger Delft ordered a Manhattan, Geneva a gin and tonic. Geneva reminded herself: this was the woman Tama said she and Thom should question.

Once the waiter turned away from their table, Inger Delft began talking and didn't appear to want to stop. "Ten years ago right here in this building I had a session all ready to go and then we got the news. I don't know if you'd be interested in my talk for your book, a revised essay? The one I was going to give before Mira—left us? I was about to pull her down from her pedestal. I thought it would be doing her a favor, showing her how to avoid getting tossed deeper into the romantic novel maelstrom. She could do so much better. It was disappointing to see her keep missing the mark—"

Geneva interrupted. "What did you suggest she should have done?"

"Deal with violence. Not skirt it. I mean people were always getting killed in her books, but so briefly. And I wanted her to allow more types of human characters in her work. She hardly let her characters leave the States. I called my talk 'The Future Mira Wallacz.' I could see where her work was headed if she took my advice, and also if she didn't. I was prepared to eviscerate the novels, point out how poorly developed, nostalgic, politically retrograde they were. Why did her work incite such—dare I say—I was actually going to use those words 'dare I say'—incite such admiration? Everything at the festival was quashed once her body was found. I never did publish the essay, although maybe I could submit it to you for the collection you and your friend are editing, if you're interested. Enough time has lapsed, I think. It's one thing to chide a living writer. It's something else altogether to confront the work of a writer who died under tragic circumstances and can't defend herself."

"Anything else you were going to say about her work?" Geneva asked.

"I was going to argue that her world-building was suggestive, slight. I thought you'd have to be weak-minded to like the novels. And then, I have to admit, seven years ago I fell into the trap. I broke my foot. The pain was intolerable, the painkillers hardly touched it, and I needed to escape. I read her posthumously published novel. All the previous novels—the ones I was going to talk about at the conference—I thought those were unreadable. But as I was saying, I was in pain, and there right by the couch were the novels I'd planned on eviscerating in public. So what did I do? I read her novels one after another. I read them in a new way, aimlessly. The funny thing: I understood her more than when I tried to read critically, analytically as a professional. The novels were all about a woman convincing herself she didn't commit a crime. She was proving something to herself. What? Maybe it was innocence? She wanted to be innocent—of some crime?"

Geneva felt her heart shift in her chest. Here was something to think about, something that could be revealing. Was Mira Wallacz guilty, and for what? And was that why her novels were popular? They were fantasies of expiation? For guilty people?

If Mira Wallacz had been murdered, was it because someone she harmed sought revenge?

Inger was continuing. "Then I made a discovery. The novels are coded. In the fifth novel the words from *To the Lighthouse* are in sequence but buried within paragraphs and set at great distances. There may be other messages."

Geneva sat back. What she would like to ask this woman: are you insane?

Inger Delft fiddled with the braid resting on her left shoulder and asked, "Did you read the last novel?"

"I read reviews."

"So you didn't actually read it. I never used to care for Mira's novels, as I've made clear, but that posthumously published one— at last she took the blinders off. It was like she was released, freed. Something must have happened to allow her to write like that, with such authority. Do you know I emailed her months before that festival with a draft of the talk I was going to give? She followed my advice to the letter in that last novel."

Geneva found this hard to believe. Surely, after reading the first disparaging sentence, the woman she imagined Mira to be would have trashed that email. She asked, "Do you have any theories about how Mira died? Do you believe it was an accident?"

Inger Delft tucked both braids over her left shoulder. "People still want it to be murder, don't they? I suppose that would be fitting. I've wondered about that—if what we write comes true. All those murders and murderers she created. Isn't it ironic that it's never been absolutely, finally determined if what happened was an accident?" She unbraided one braid, looped the elastic band around her thumb. "She was very cruel to women in her fiction. I mean, she was like Joyce Carol Oates in that way—she tortures women and girls in fiction and leaves them in suspension with more horrors to come. Women are basically prey animals in Mira's novels, with fewer survival instincts than baby bunnies. I mean, Mira covered up her sadism by making sure that the murderer wasn't a woman and that a woman discovers the truth and administers justice. Okay, but the inciting event in novel after novel focuses on horrors visited upon a woman. What does the ending matter when there's always a woman's corpse dragged through the plot?"

Geneva was very glad she ordered a gin and tonic. Her glass was nearly empty. And really, why should she have needed Thom to help her conduct interviews? It's hard to get people to stop talking, actually. She might as well be bold and push toward the obvious question. Inger Delft, after all, was uncorked. "If Mira was murdered," Geneva asked, "do you have any idea who might have done it?"

"Oh dear. It could have been anyone. I've always wondered why more people weren't hounded by detectives. It's like the local police didn't want to discover the truth. Maybe it's a local who did it? I'd venture a possibility, but I don't really know anyone in this area. Nor would I want to, from what Tama wrote in the biography. A lot of people had suspicions about Mira. She was like Shirley Jackson in that way. Surrounded by people who didn't understand her and suspected her. Not that they thought she was a witch, apparently.

Not like what the crummy townspeople thought about Shirley Jackson. It's just that Mira was generally disliked—that's what I heard and Tama's biography confirms it. Well, that happens to plenty of artists. People can't stand them once they get to know them."

Geneva searched her memory before she said, "I read Tama Squires's biography, but I don't remember anything you're telling me."

"Oh it's there," Inger Delft said, finishing off her drink. "Resentment. You can read it between the lines. Just little digs. Tama Squires must have hated doing the real research, and so she didn't focus much on Mira's upbringing. I've always wondered about Tama Squires, if she knows more than she's telling. That wife of hers. A rumor went around that she was a contract killer. Seriously."

"Lizette? You mean she was contracted to kill someone?"

"It's just gossip."

"That's pretty terrible gossip," Geneva said.

"I know. That's what makes it so interesting."

"You don't believe it."

"What does belief have to do with anything? If you listen to gossip, Tama and Lizette are much more interesting, aren't they? I wouldn't be surprised if Lizette got drunk and conked Tama on the head and left her in the woods and couldn't remember the spot and that's why she went around moaning that Tama was missing. She's trying to cover her tracks. Their arguments are notorious."

"Was Lizette here ten years ago?"

"Possibly, although maybe she's a more recent acquisition."

Feeling fraudulent, Geneva gave Inger Delft her email and the deadline for contributing to the collection—which probably would never be assembled or published, after all. She hadn't texted Thom

Crystl and if he texted her she didn't think she would reply. Still, she checked her phone. No messages.

Geneva was back in her room when Aida called. She sounded strange, rushed, her voice high. "I keep having bad dreams and you're in them," she said. "Elson wanted me to check on you. He's worried."

"Elson? He's heartless."

"I've been meaning to tell you—we've been getting along."

"This is Elson you're talking about?"

Aida was silent for so long that Geneva guessed the truth. "Aida, you're seeing him. Elson? He was always threatening to fire you."

"We'd been having quarrels, and he thought maybe we were taking things too far."

Geneva lay back on the bed. "My god, he'll fire us both—he'll keep firing us. Wait. Now I guess he can't. You can blackmail him. What about Stacey? I thought you loved her."

"I do. Elson loves her too. It's so complex and so—alive. But it can't last in the current formulation. Stacey has to go. Do I sound disloyal?"

"Yes."

"You don't understand about Stacey and the kind of person she is. I used to like that sort of person, you know the kind you can bounce off of. Like they can't be affected and can't be changed? She was very—contained—and then she wasn't and neither was I. It's satisfying to make someone lose their bearings. Stacey and I had that—we made each other lose our bearings. It's basically psychotic. She couldn't feel or even think very far into our relationship and neither could I. A real curb on the imagination. I thought Stacey cared about me—because of the way she smiled at me. That smile

157

wasn't special at all. She had to practice that smile in her rear view mirror. For years. She thinks Elson is just a quivering bucket of a person because he acts all authoritarian on everybody when he's really tender-hearted and wobbly, jelly wobbly. He's actually a lot like Stacey under the skin. You put them together and it would be one big ugly puddle."

"So now you're with Elson and no one else, not Stacey?"

"Yes, and so? But that's not what I called you about. I keep wondering about Thom Crystl and if he has bad intentions. It's just—I worry."

"Don't worry."

Aida huffed. "I still wonder if meeting Thom Crystl at that party might not be a coincidence. That possibility has never faded away for me. Maybe he really was following you. Maybe he thinks you know something about what happened to Mira that could cause problems for him."

"It's been ten years, Aida. If I 'know something' I would have remembered it by now. You were the one who told me that wacky clarinet story. By the way, he's leaving me to my own devices."

"What do you mean?"

"He won't help anymore. He doesn't believe in what we're doing."

"Well, what are you doing? What have you found out?"

"Not much. Except that everyone I talk to has a motive. Maybe I'm the real problem. In the mood I'm in everyone seems capable of murder."

Aida sighed and the phone whistled. "You're just finding this out? I keep reminding you that we're a murderous species, Geneva."

⁑ CHAPTER SEVENTEEN

T HE PORTRAIT'S EYES glinted with a suggestion of mischief, to the right of the mouth a teasing lift at the corner. The lips, pink-red, looked like a deflated heart. The neck was oddly long, and at the throat's base: an infantilizing Peter Pan blouse collar. That collar was something from too many decades ago. The artist had torn Mira Wallacz from her own generation, settled her in an earlier era.

"Not a very good likeness, is it?" A scent of mint toothpaste, hand sanitizer, and something floral. "Of course you don't know that if you've never met her. Photographs never did her justice." An older woman in a sweater too large for her had appeared beside Geneva.

"Didn't they?" Geneva said. She turned back to the painting and focused, this time, on the background. An altar rose behind Mira Wallacz's face—no—a hill, rounded, a wash of green and brown. On each side, in ascending order: stones.

A scribble at the base, an illegible signature. By the time Geneva turned to gauge the stranger's reaction to the portrait, the woman had disappeared. Only her perfume lingered. The scent was recognizable now: lily of the valley.

At the reception table in the lobby Geneva asked the cheerful-looking man in enormous glasses if he knew who painted Mira Wallacz's portrait.

"Wait. I'll find out."

As he consulted his phone, Geneva craned toward the elevators, looking for Thom Crystl. He could at least have told her when he was leaving. Or let her know if he already left.

The man looked up again—he was as beautiful as a male model, high cheekbones, dark rimmed eyes behind his glasses. "Oakley Beals. He donated the portrait to the conference to raise funds. I don't suppose you're interested in buying it?"

Geneva felt her face heat. She was going to have to lie. "I'd like to meet the artist first. Before buying. Is that possible? I could see him? Would that be all right?"

"Okay. We'll call and ask. You're not joking about buying it? Be kind, okay?"

Geneva was opening her Uber app when a bus pulled to the curb. She took the seat behind the driver and felt a wash of unreality. Years ago, when the center was brand new, a bus had deposited her just down the road. She had walked the rest of the way to the center, past birches and maples and enormous oaks. She'd been tempted to go into the woods, the dark woods that looked inviting. But now? Not now.

Oakley Beals's flannel shirt was sheared off to his shoulders, the material unraveling. His arms were heavily muscled, like those of a much younger man. He settled down in a recliner that was pushed back almost to the sink. Paper cups, takeout boxes, apple cores littered the counter under the window behind him. Geneva took the spindly-backed chair opposite him.

He caught her glance at the counter. "I had a party with friends. I'm feeling it now." He sighed heavily. "Arthritis, it's a sneaky bitch. Inflammation. Start eating salmon. Lift weights. Build your upper body. Get your fish oil. I'm taking new stuff they tried out on horses. It doesn't work as well as it should. Then again, last time I looked I'm not a horse."

He stretched, pivoting his shoulders, and opened the window. Cool air circulated. Geneva took a breath that finally wasn't shallow.

She complimented him on the portrait. "The eyes—you captured something. I couldn't stop looking."

"You were a friend of Mira's, or just an admirer?" he asked.

"I met her only once. Even so, it was evident you captured something of her spirit."

He cleared his throat. "What would you know about her spirit if you met her only once?"

Geneva's stomach tightened. "I felt like I knew her—from her books. I read her books since I was a kid. First the children's books. By the time I was twelve I was reading her novels."

Oakley Beals sat back, his gaze softening. "Good for you. Well, I'm glad the portrait has meaning for you at least. I know that the organizers aren't too pleased by it. They forget that I can read faces really well. They don't think it will sell."

"I don't see why they'd have a problem."

"People always have problems."

The room felt close again, despite the open window. She said, "Mira Wallacz didn't seem like she had many problems."

"You really didn't know her." His grin was sour, contemptuous. "You wouldn't know about her problems."

"To paint her portrait—you must have known her well to capture her spirit. It takes an incredible amount of patience and skill, I imagine." She feared she was flattering him so much that he'd suspect her. She went on. "What I said about Mira and problems. I know we all have problems. She must have poured hers into her novels. To get rid of them, the problems, I mean." Her voice was weakening. She clasped her hands together to keep herself from rising up out of the chair and running to the door. She shouldn't be here, flattering this man, pretending she would buy his abominable art.

Oakley Beals drew himself up. He was either going to tell her to leave or regale her. "I knew her since she was a child and she always attracted problems. It's amazing she wrote anything, given how little help she had. Well, she came so far with no support. Oh, she had her mother, a lot of good it did her. That mother of hers didn't like her own daughter. A child can feel that lack of love and Mira was a sensitive person. Naturally, she loved her mother—people denied love will still love and try to be loved. Wrote those children's books under her own name and wouldn't let anyone know she wrote the novels. Couldn't face Eileen's disapproval. When those novels came out and Mira's name was attached to them Eileen was embarrassed by her own daughter. Found the books slutty. Didn't plump up her own reputation. Eileen didn't want Mira to have so much power. Not to tell tales but, you know, I don't think Mira was forgiven until Eileen was dying."

"How do you know?" Geneva asked gently.

"I was Mira's friend. And it's all over the books. Mira's problems, they were always there in the books, disguised. She really didn't believe she was forgiven by her mother for just being who she was."

"Everything changed when her mother was ill? She was for-given?"

Oakley Beals cleared his throat. "She didn't need to be forgiven. It was Eileen who was guilty and should have begged for forgive-ness. Eileen wasn't interested in her daughter for years, was disap-pointed, had other fish to fry—cared more for those neighbor kids, those Kleist boys than for her own child. Cared more for those boys' mother too. It didn't go by Mira—her mother's disappointment in her. You can smell that a mile off."

A gust parted the curtains and Oakley Beals turned and shut the window.

"Why did Mira's mother like the neighbors? I don't under-stand."

"Terri Kleist made a terrific flying monkey, doing whatever Eileen wanted. Admiration was what Eileen wanted. She had a rep-utation as a very good person, charitable, a friend to all. People will do a lot to maintain that sort of reputation. And when the novels came out and Mira's name eventually got revealed as the author and the interviews started, Eileen had to believe she was in danger of losing her own good reputation by raising such a daughter. Local people saw themselves in those books too—their speech patterns, clothing choices. Well, Mira was smart enough to show them who they were. And then there was all that stuff that came out eventu-ally on social media and that riled up people too. It's not true that you can never go home again. You can never leave home again." He chuckled, and Geneva was sure he had longed for this opportunity to talk about Mira Wallacz. She just had to be quiet and attentive and he would tell her more than anyone else had.

He chewed his lip, shifted in his chair. "People will always have theories about her. Mira should have been more distressed about what came up online—the fake accounts. She tried to have them taken down a couple of times but just gave up. It happens to a lot of celebrities. Somebody posted absolutely vile things—like she said those things. Terrible things about people in Bingle. To enhance her reputation, being mean-spirited but funny to get people to pay attention to her. That's what people thought she was up to."

"You're talking about Facebook or—?"

"Instagram too, the early days when people didn't know what they were doing. Whoever did it got photos of her and used her name and doctored some other photos, although a number of those photos, I know for a fact, were real. People thought she was showing off her wealth. I couldn't resist looking after a while. At least I figured out that the accounts weren't genuine even before Mira told me."

"Who made the fake accounts? Do you have theories?"

He sniffed as if she'd insulted him. "Obviously I have theories. Any obsessed fan could have done it, except the thing was: some of those photos were from Mira's childhood. And those photos weren't available online otherwise. Now who would have had those photos? I used to bet it was someone who knew her mother. Or even her mother was somehow involved maybe. The problem with people like Eileen Wallacz, people who seem so kind, so nice— people like that have all sorts of excuses for what they do. You can count on their having a wicked side like everybody else, except it's harder for them to control that side of themselves. They've invested far too much energy in trying to convince everyone of their virtue. Besides, they're so sure about their own goodness they can even fool themselves. Eileen didn't have the technical ability to post anything much online, I'm betting. But she could have given photos to somebody, just to teach Mira a lesson."

"Wouldn't that defeat her purpose? If she was already embarrassed by Mira, why would she want to post images that could be even more embarrassing?"

"I imagine if Eileen did it she thought Mira would eventually want to give up writing the sorts of novels she wrote—that Mira would feel guilty because it was evident that people were hurt by those novels. Or maybe Eileen just enjoyed seeing people's reactions. At first she was embarrassed, but maybe later she fed off the whole mess. Eileen was always complicated that way. Jealous, you know? If anyone was going to be in control of Mira's reputation she wanted to be the one—and the attention it gave Eileen, the pity and the attention, maybe in a perverse way that could have felt good, I suppose."

"Quite a few people thought that the accounts were real?" Geneva said.

Oakley Beals smacked his lips. "There are always idiots, aren't there? I suspect you might be one of them?" He smiled. It was clear he enjoyed teasing, trying to get a rise out of her.

She ignored the insult. "I never saw what was posted—it's just what I heard."

"Whoever made the sites you heard about took them down hours after the news came out that Mira died. That tells you something too—that it wasn't Mira who made the accounts."

"Mira complained to you about all this?"

"She used to visit. Probably pity visits, thinking she was helping an old guy out. I didn't care if they were pity visits. It was nice to see her. Of course she complained about the online lies. Laughed about them too. Probably they didn't hurt her sales. She didn't believe me when I told her my suspicions that Eileen meant to embarrass her and gave photos of her away to be posted. The fact is: Mira didn't understand her own mother and what she was capable of. I think if Eileen was involved with any online hoax it's mainly, like I said, because she wanted attention too—decided after the initial embarrassment that she might as well cooperate with whoever was posting that stuff and get that person's attention. Maybe she could get her revenge on the town and still feel blameless and get people's pity for having such an ungrateful daughter. Mira didn't understand her mother and her mother didn't understand her or herself."

"And you did?" Geneva didn't mean for her voice to sound like a challenge.

Oakley Beals tented his fingers over his stomach. He looked pleased to accept a challenge. "Years ago copies of a letter went around in the mail to various people. No return address, no signature. Posted from another county. That letter made clear what one of the more well-regarded women in Bingle was doing in the backroom of the post office. Now who would know that? Other than someone who worked at the post office. Eileen always denied sending that letter. I knew her phrasing, knew it was her. I went to school with Eileen—I knew what she was capable of, bless her soul. That's why I think she was out to play a trick on her own daughter. It seemed obvious that she was playing tricks again, that maybe she was letting someone get ahold of old photos of Mira. People don't forget about Mira and they still don't forgive either."

"That was so long ago," Geneva said. "Now they're both gone— Mira and her mother. It's been a decade. Why would anyone in town hold a grudge? It's all so sad."

"You think people want to forget? It feels too damn good to be affronted. It got worse after Mira died. Because then she leaves everything she has to the younger Kleist boy who was the parish priest that year—can you imagine? I'll say this—the church looks nice, and they added a food pantry and a parish hall and the new priest has as many as three bathrooms. The Kleist boy just up and got away from the priesthood. Just took off. Mira's death must have been a shock to his system. Or she woke him up. God knows. Though it's not all a sad story. In the last months of her life Mira got her mother back. I don't know why Eileen came to her senses, but she tried to make it up to Mira. Didn't like her neighbor Terri Kleist so much by then. Stopped seeing Terri, that's why it shocked everyone when Mira gave her money to Terri's younger boy. Eileen should have figured something was wrong with that Kleist family from the beginning and so should have Mira. I wasn't surprised when those Kleist boys entered the seminary. They needed to get away."

"From their family?"

"And from the whole lousy area. Too many rumors."

"What rumors?"

He grinned. Aida had been right—people are hungry to be heard, especially lonely people. "You're full of questions, aren't you? I don't blame you. I've always been full of questions myself." He stared hard at her before he went on. "The rumors were about the dad—the Kleist boys' dad. It's been a long time, though I still recall what happened, mostly. The dad died—hitting his head, tripping on the cellar steps. Everyone thought there was more to it. Like one of the boys was horsing around and pushed his dad. Or Terri Kleist herself shoved her husband and didn't want people to know, so she blamed Mira. Terri let it be known that her husband fell because Mira came flouncing into the house wearing a wet bathing suit and made the cellar steps slippery. Mira went over to the house because her mother had to have a jar of canned peaches, borrowing from the Kleists. Well, Terri was the one who sent Mira down the stairs in her wet bathing suit. The next thing you know the boys' father slips and hits his head. And Mira never got over it."

He was silent for nearly a minute before he blinked again and again, as if waking and realizing he wasn't alone. "Did you want to know more about the portrait? Did you come here for anything else? About the price?"

"I have a question about the stones along the rim of the face. In the portrait."

"What stones?"

"Along the rim in the painting, by Mira Wallacz's head—on each side of her head."

"You're telling me they stuck stones beside the portrait?"

Baffled, Geneva said, "No, I mean. In your painting. The paintings of stones there. I think people might be puzzled because of the manner of her death."

"There are no stones in the painting."

"What did I see then?"

"You should have seen steps—steps ascending, steps up the hillside. People don't know how to look. How to see."

He started to stand. His legs trembled from the effort. When he spoke again, his voice shook with anger. "They're steps, one for each of those novels. Good god. You wanted to buy the portrait and you think it's about the stones that killed her? I wouldn't sell you that portrait for a million dollars."

Geneva hurried from the house, not knowing where she was going, only that she wanted to get far away from where Oakley Beals could see her from his windows.

The stones were "steps" he had said. Maybe he'd intended as much, but the unconscious always "speaks"—something one of her professors used to say. Could Oakley Beals have murdered Mira Wallacz? He hardly seemed strong enough to traipse through the woods. But ten years ago? Had Oakley Beals once thought Mira Wallacz remembered him in her will, out of the pity he believed she had for him?

Oakley Beals's speculations about Mira's guilt for the accident with Thom's father—Geneva felt dizzy with this new possibility and what it meant. The symmetry of Mira's death with the death of Thom's father: a wound to the head. Mira went down the stairs in her wet bathing suit before Thom's father presumably slipped. But Oakley Beals said there were rumors that one of the boys or even Thom's mother—Terri Kleist—was responsible. That might be the actual truth. Yet Terri Kleist told the story in a way that put all blame on Mira. What if, years afterward, Mira discovered that the death of Thom's father hadn't been her fault after all? Wouldn't she have been enraged?

The fact that Mira and her mother were—finally—close, that was something Thom made clear too. Eileen's illness would account for that: she depended on her daughter, her need for her daughter changed her attitude. Eileen Wallacz's closeness to Terri Kleist had suffered damage by then. Had she known that Terri Kleist blamed Mira? Had she initially blamed Mira too and taken Terri's word about Mira's guilt? For how long? Or did she finally believe another version of what happened to Thom's father and stopped talking to her neighbor? Or was there an entirely different explanation for the death of Thom Crystl's father?

Geneva's phone pinged with a text. It had to be Thom Crystl at last. Their parting—maybe she had made too much of what he said. It would be good to talk to him, to tell him what she'd found out from Oakley Beals. To see if it all made sense to him. To find out the truth about what happened on the cellar stairs.

No message, only a photo. Blurred. She enlarged the image, made note of the pale green doorway framing the photo. It had to be at the conference center, near the bank of windows that looked toward the lake. Tama was there, younger and larger than she was now, and squeezed behind her were other bodies, other faces. Difficult to make them out. Towering above them all, the top of his head cut off but the rest of his face recognizable: Thom Crystl.

He had lied when he said he wasn't at the festival ten years ago. The photo proved it.

She kept walking, pausing only to check for directions on her phone.

⸻ CHAPTER EIGHTEEN

T HE SMELL OF INCENSE tickled Geneva's throat. A statue of
Mary, the pale lips open, as if about to speak, hovered in an
alcove. Geneva believed she was alone—and then, echoing
steps.

"Can I help you?"

This couldn't possibly be Thom's brother, could it? There was
no resemblance. And she remembered: his brother had his own
parish in California.

"I was looking for information about Father Kleist?" she said.

"The first or the second?" The priest sounded good-natured, at
ease, mildly curious about her. This was the house of the Lord and
he belonged.

"The one who's still a priest?" she said.

"Oh yes. You can find him in San Diego, at Our Lady of Perpet-
ual Help. Just try online and the site pops right up. Are you a rela-
tive? Or you used to be a parishioner and remember him and his
brother? I'd know you if you were a regular."

"I'm an acquaintance of Thom's, the other brother."

"That's nice. I can't say that I know him very well. He's only
been by once since I've been here. By all reports he's a good man.
What he left to the parish surprised everyone. He took the vow of
poverty seriously. At least he honored one vow."

Such a chatty, gossipy priest. She had no idea priests could be this way—so terribly human.

"A couple others like you visited us," he said, staring at her forehead and then into her eyes. "Some of them thought he was still a priest. But you—maybe you were sent here for spiritual reasons?"

"I'm with the conference. You heard about what's going on at the conference center, honoring Mira Wallacz, the writer?"

He nodded, his eyes shining. "Her passing—people still talk about that. We've had head wound deaths for years around here. My neighbor slipped on the stairs of her porch and cracked her skull open. A woman named Jean Shepps—maybe you read about her?—hit her head on a beam at the park. Couldn't remember afterwards what happened. The swing set had been disassembled and was perched on its side and somehow she must have walked right into it. People found her because her baby's stroller rolled down the hill there and somebody filmed that baby stroller tearing down the hill without the mother. The baby was fine. It went viral—that video. And there was a girl on a rock pile. She slid off after she fell asleep with her friend. At first the police thought she suffered from snake bite because of the snakes always curling up in that pile. When they moved her body they saw where a rock struck her—it must have tumbled down, that rock, from the top of the pile to do that kind of damage. It happens too often, doesn't it?" Abruptly, he changed the subject. "Do you know many of our parishioners?"

"I did meet someone who's local. Do you know the artist, Oakley Beals?"

The priest grinned, shook his head. "Oh—Oakley. Sad about the arthritis. It hit him about five years ago. Before then you'd see him jogging around like an Olympic athlete. Knew every shrub. Mr. Flora and Fauna. Grew herbs. He drifted away from the church, said he found his religion in the great outdoors. Makes good dandelion wine, I'll give him that. Could name every tree and weed in the forest too. A regular naturalist." He paused, looked at something behind Geneva, before he said, "A woman was here the other day from that festival—or is it a conference? Whatever it is. Maybe you knew her? She's your friend, possibly?"

"Did you catch her name?"

"I can't say as I did. She was very nice. I don't know as she even gave her name. Could you be here to bolster your own faith?"

"I was just—I want to know more about the Kleist brothers. You've been in the parish for a long time?"

"Only the last three years. I wish I could tell you more. Perhaps you're really here for other reasons—your own faith. The woman who was here yesterday had questions too."

Words rang from behind Geneva. "She was old!" The shout came from a man wearing a short-sleeved plaid shirt, his pale hair falling past his shoulders in a greasy cape. He stepped closer. His eyes: a deep swimming dark brown with whites all around. Protruding eyes.

"Everyone looks old to someone as young as you two," the priest said. "I wouldn't say she was all that old. But pleasant. With questions about both Father Kleists."

"She didn't say why she wanted to know about them?" Geneva asked.

"Oh no. I wouldn't pry like that. I've always thought that asking too many questions amounts to rudeness. I'm from the Midwest. It may be a habit or a predilection picked up from living so long in that part of the country." When Geneva didn't respond, he said, "It was nice talking to you. I have to attend to a few things." He was dismissing her and seemed a bit sheepish, realizing he'd been garrulous.

She took out her phone, showed him the photograph. "Do you recognize him?" she asked.

"Certainly. He's so young here that I almost didn't know who he was. That's one of the Kleists, isn't it? That has to be the younger one, or maybe not?"

When Geneva stepped outside, the man who had shouted was running a hose down the church's steps, the water streaming. "Be careful," he called to her. "It's wet. You need to be careful."

She turned away and the skin on her back shuddered. She was sure he was still watching her.

⊬ CHAPTER NINETEEN

I N HER HOTEL ROOM Geneva unscrewed another of the mini wine bottles that Aida had tucked into her satchel. If she weren't so exhausted she would open her sketchbook and try to draw her way toward clarity.

She had hoped the priest might be helpful, not disappointing and confusing. The photograph taken years ago might have been of Thom or of his older brother George. If she asked Thom about the photograph—when she was ready, after she did some more thinking, and assuming he would talk to her—she wouldn't mention his brother George. She'd let him believe she was sure it was him. Let him answer for the photograph. If it was his image he would have to explain why he didn't tell her he was at the festival ten years ago. And if the photograph was of George?

Between the curtains in her room a lightning streak turned the sky a brilliant purple before darkness blotted out everything and then—a sizzling sound, a warning, and thunder pounded.

A sip for each thunder clap. Time to slow down, Geneva told herself. She didn't feel like rehearsing murder suspects again. She'd done enough of that. She couldn't wait any longer to confront Thom, wherever he was.

After she opened the third mini bottle she called him without expecting an answer.

Thom answered before the second ring.

"You're still here?" she asked.

"Of course. I wouldn't leave you."

"You didn't call me."

"Did you call me? I missed it. I had a feeling you weren't in the mood to talk to me for a while—after I disappointed you."

She kept her voice steady. "I'm coming to your room. I have questions for you."

He laughed. "Questions?"

As she came off the elevator he was already at his door, holding it open. He was smiling before he saw her glare. She wished her eyes gave off heat. Once inside his room she went to the armchair near the desk. Across from her he settled on another hard-backed chair, his forehead knotted.

She began. "You were here. You were at the conference center when Mira Wallacz was here. Ten years ago."

"Why do you say that?"

She showed him her phone. She suspected he'd deny it was him. The photograph was blurred, after all.

"I was," he admitted at last. "That's true."

She was so surprised she coughed. She bent her head, put her hands over her eyes.

When she pulled her hands away she said, "You didn't tell the police. You were supposed to be at the church. That's what you told them. Why?"

He raised his hands then dropped them to his lap. "You have to understand what my brother was going through. Later he was exonerated, but at the time false allegations had been made against him. He had been unable for nearly a year to officiate while his case was being investigated by the diocese. He went ahead without my knowing what he was going to do. It was something he felt urged to do by his own conscience, by his belief that the parish-ioners needed to hear Mass when I left to find Mira. Another priest was coming in to substitute for me—but there was trouble and he couldn't make it. George took the call about the cancelation. I didn't know he had filled in until later. What would happen to George if it was known he was officiating Mass? If I had told anyone what he had done he would have been in grave trouble. That level of disobedience wouldn't be tolerated. I don't think you can under-stand. He was also called Father Kleist, and we looked enough alike that parishioners—many of them well over eighty—couldn't tell the difference."

Geneva wished she hadn't had anything to drink. Nevertheless, she was growing more sober by the minute. She asked, "You really haven't answered me. Why were you at the conference center?"

"Mira left a message for me to meet her. Whoever took the mes-sage got the time wrong. I was supposed to meet her in town. I must have been late—I missed her. When she didn't show up I came here to the conference center where I thought I could find her. I knew I might not get back in time for the Mass and so that's why I had a substitute—but, as I said, that didn't work out. My brother filled in for me. It was a day of—getting things wrong."

"Why did Mira want to see you?"

"I've never figured that out. I wish I knew."

Geneva's chest was beginning to ache. "Your brother has an al-ibi and you don't," she said. "You could have told me the truth. If what you're saying is actually true. You didn't trust me."

He was silent, motionless.

She went on. "So you're not going to contradict me. Okay. You didn't trust me and still don't. You were here on the day Mira was killed and you lied about it to the police to protect your brother and yourself. Lied about it to me too. You're maybe guilty about that or about more than that? Guilt—that's what haunts you? And haunted Mira too? Does that make any sense to you? Was there any reason for Mira to feel guilty about you? I talked to Oakley Beals. He told me about how Mira was blamed for what happened to your father."

Thom reached his hand out toward hers. She pulled away before he could touch her. "I don't blame you for what you're suggesting," he said. "Listen. What happened with my father was an accident. The two of us boys had been on one of those slip-and-slide mats. Mira came over—she was picking up something for her mother. I guess my mother wanted to give Eileen's mother something from the basement. Mira joined me and George, just playing around. The steps down to the cellar were old wood, painted glossy. She was wet from the slip-and-slide and tracking in water. My father followed her down the steps. He must have slipped. You know how stoic that generation of men were. He was fine, he claimed, just a little banged up. Went to bed that night with a headache. My mother never had been able to get him to go to the doctor, he wasn't about to go that night. When she woke up the next morning he was dead next to her."

"I'm so sorry, Thom."

"I'm sorry Mira felt she had to bear any guilt."

Footsteps rushed outside in the hall. She waited for them to pass before she asked, "Did your brother blame Mira? Did you—at least for a while?"

"Never. George and I loved that she got wet on that stupid toy that day. My dad might have slipped anyway. His balance was terrible by then, and he drank. My mother never liked to admit that. They both drank. After my dad died Mira kind of hid herself for a while. Even from my brother and me. Believe me, we never blamed her. She couldn't understand that. She thought she was to blame for anything that happened to us, anything we lost because of our father's death. And then later when it came out that she'd written those novels, Eileen—Eileen was her mother—Eileen was furious with her, but Mira still stuck with her mother, visiting her, trying to please her. Eileen didn't know how to show love to Mira until about a year before she died—before Eileen died, I mean—and then things changed that year. You could feel it in the house."

"You visited them?"

"Just a few times. As a priest. Eileen had at-home hospice. Mira was taking care of her. She didn't want me to continue as a priest but she wanted me to visit, to pray with Eileen. Eileen died only three months before Mira's own death."

"Did Mira's death influence your choice to leave the priesthood?"

"It was already beginning to happen. I knew I shouldn't be a leader or in service work of that sort. Even George knew that about me. Mira tried to convince me that I was simply following George, that the priesthood wasn't my genuine vocation. My mother felt the same way when I brought it up. I suppose I was avoiding failure as a poet, avoiding what I should have been doing all along. And Mira— I should have told her as much. Her dying was a shock. Everything was cracked open. I realized how much she meant to me."

"You were in love with her?"

"No. Though I think George was—I think she may have had more to do with why he became a priest than he'd ever admit."

Geneva thought of what Oakley Beals had said about Eileen Wallacz. "Thom, you never noticed anything wrong about Mira's mother—before those last months of her life?"

He pressed his hands together. "When I was a kid I thought Mira's mother had the meanest eyes I'd ever seen. I told that to my mother once and she slapped my back so hard that I hit my chin on the kitchen table and cut my tongue. I never saw Mira's mother actually do anything unkind. It was a kid thing, a kid's perception. I wanted Mira's mother to be evil because I liked Mira and Mira seemed unhappy. George and I used to pretend to rescue her. We wanted her to be in trouble so we could rescue her. I guess that's why I created a fantasy about her mother being this half-evil sort of person."

"What if you were right?"

"I wasn't. I saw them together during the last months and Eileen's eyes—they were very kind. She radiated love for her daughter."

"Maybe what you saw as a child was real too? Thom, Mira confessed to you, didn't she? What did she tell you about the accident on the steps?"

"I can't tell you that—even though I'm no longer a priest. What happened when my father had his accident—I don't want to dwell on that either."

What was Geneva supposed to think? If Thom didn't fully trust her, and she knew he didn't, Geneva also knew another truth: she could no longer trust him, not entirely.

"Thom, why did you really leave the priesthood?"

He laid his hands flat on his thighs as if holding himself down in his chair.

She waited.

At last he said, "I kept having anxiety attacks, hallucinating. After Mira's death I blamed myself. I should have been with her. Like I said, someone at the parish took her message over the phone and I misread the note or else that person got it all wrong. Afterwards when I learned what happened to her it was like my mind and body wouldn't. . . . I couldn't tell what was real and what wasn't. I didn't sleep for days. The panic attacks got worse. I'd had them since I was about eleven years old, but these were worse. Waves of them.

I didn't know who I was, couldn't help anyone. Couldn't help myself. I was breaking down, sobbing like a kid for hours. And I was ashamed of myself. To be so weak. The only thing that helped was when I made a plan to get rid of the past. Changing my name, leaving the priesthood—to expunge the past and start again. I'd failed Mira, I'd taken a vow I didn't believe in. I had nothing to fall back on. And Mira gave me everything she had. That was a burden. I wish she'd given the money to anyone else. Coming here brings it all back. I didn't want to come. I shouldn't have."

Geneva softened her voice. "Why did you come?"

"For you."

After a pause she said, "I think I need some time alone—to think about all this."

"We're alike," he said. "We need lots of time to think, and we have to be alone to do it. I understand."

In her room Geneva asked herself if she was already making excuses for Thom Crystl. He loved his brother, could not expose his brother for officiating Mass when George was directly forbidden to do so by the diocese. Thom was only being protective, she let herself imagine. And although initially Mira Wallacz and her mother and Thom's own mother had discouraged him from becoming a priest, Thom had finally been a spiritual adviser to both Mira and her mother. Or maybe that was going too far. He visited, he said. He didn't think he'd done much good. Of course that was how he felt about everything.

Shouldn't his vulnerability, his willingness to let Geneva know what he suffered, that he failed, that he had endured panic attacks and hallucinations, shouldn't that suggest he trusted Geneva—as a friend? It wasn't weak to change one's life, for him to reject the pressure to remain in the priesthood. To be ridiculed and accept it. Maybe he had helped Mira and her mother after all. No doubt he told Mira she had nothing to be guilty about for his father's death. But hadn't Thom and his brother George been blamed? That was a rumor that Oakley Beals told her about. Or their mother had been guilty. Oakley Beals even suggested that Terri Kleist might have pushed her own husband on the steps and blamed Mira.

Mira had enemies and she might not have known who they were. The only reason Geneva knew that Mira had enemies was because ten years ago she had observed, listened, heard an undertone in other voices. She heard because she was expecting the opposite: love, admiration. What we don't expect, that's what we notice. And why hadn't she noticed that Thom was at the festival back then? She'd never seen him then, not once. Perhaps he'd seen her.

Whom could Geneva trust? Maybe she depended too much on trust ever since she was a child. A memory came for her. Sixth grade. A terrible winter. Wearing her red raincoat, too flimsy and thin, and red rubber boots that froze and turned hard and could hardly be pulled off, her socks coming off with them. She wanted to stand by her teacher on the playground. For warmth. But the look the pretty teacher gave her, the disgust on her face, made Mira see herself—her clothes too short and wrong for the weather, her bangs stuck to her forehead. That afternoon on her way home from school, she made a promise to herself while a mud puddle crackled under her red rubber boots. Pulling her boots from the cataract of ice, she vowed to give everyone chance after chance after chance in her own life, not to judge, not ever.

When she was older and attracted the notice of boys and men this was revealed as a horrible pledge. She tried to trust even when her instincts told her to run. Maybe not only the pledge was to blame: Mira Wallacz was at fault too, and Geneva's naïve reading of those floatingly beautiful romances. The author's primary characters also put their faith in the wrong people and yet, for them, things worked out. So unlike actual human experience. Books can't be your only guide to life, Geneva learned. Not that there were other guides much more reliable.

She could judge herself as naïve. It's possible, with time, to get more naive. Ideas. More ideas can make anyone stupid. You can reason away anything.

She had to admit: probably Thom Crystl came with her to the conference center because she had wanted him to. He was easily swayed, the sort of person who can be made to do whatever a stronger personality proposes. Or he came out of charitable instincts. Or because he had for years distrusted himself.

After Geneva was back in her room, Aida called. Her first words: "You found the murderer yet?"

"Hello to you too. Is everything all right?"

"Sure. I was just curious. You found the murderer, didn't you?"

"You actually believe that's possible. I used to believe that too."

Aida made a noise that was half-sniff, half-sneeze. "It's not a lost cause, though, is it?" she asked. "At least you must be meeting some interesting people, I hope? I've been missing you when I'm not worried to death about you. By the way, I finally read part of a Mira Wallacz novel. The one about the despicable real estate agent. I usually only like books that teach me something new—like metallurgy or strategic defenses in the Crimean War, but I didn't learn much about real estate. I'd like to unlearn the sex scenes. They're like badminton. A lot of useless, lightweight action. What do they call the thing that you hit in badminton?"

"A shuttlecock."

"Exactly."

Geneva told her friend that she'd return home the next night. She'd catch an Uber to the train station in Waverly.

"I'll pick you up."

"I'd like that," Geneva said. "In fact, I'd love that. I've really missed you."

"You don't mind that Elson will be coming along? His car's more reliable than mine."

Geneva laughed. "I really have to see this side of him—the side you like."

"I never said I liked him. I'm training him to be likeable and he's doing the same with me, I suppose."

Oh no, Geneva thought. One of those relationships that "takes work." Aida would be on strike any day now.

Chapter Twenty

In the morning the easel that had held Mira Wallacz's portrait was empty, and Geneva felt the unexpected sting of loss. She almost wished she owned the painting, or at least had taken a photograph. The attempt to see the image in her memory taunted her. Why had what she thought she saw differed so dramatically from the artist's intention—if Oakley Beals was telling the truth?

When Geneva asked where the painting was, the woman behind the registration desk looked up, her eyebrows rising. "The artist came in a huff and took it away. Just as well. Some woman said she wanted to buy it and never came up with the cash."

The skylight over the pool gave off dim light from the overcast day. The only other guest was a man in a lounge chair with his head sunk over his laptop. An older woman joined the man, kicked at his ankle to get him to notice her, sat down and read from her phone.

Geneva swam with slow strokes. When she rose from the water she hurried to the lounge chair where she left her towel. The rough feel of the fabric was wonderful. Stephanie Binks must have slipped in from the entrance near the outdoor pool. She was sitting at a patio table, leaning back, chin raised, motionless.

Geneva spoke before she could lose her nerve. "Have you heard how Tama's doing?"

The agent looked up. "They're keeping her overnight again. It's a mild concussion. The moral: don't walk in the dark and crash into a low-hanging branch."

"How is Lizette taking it?"

"Hysterically. Tama is fine, and well enough to complain. That hard head of hers. I don't think anyone could damage it much."

Geneva's hair was dripping on her shoulders. She felt exposed, wet and shivering, despite her towel. "You're not going to swim?" she asked.

Stephanie Binks grinned. "I come to the pool when I want to get away from everyone. They're not the most athletic group here. Not many swimmers. Usually no one bothers me. I'm safe—or so I thought."

Geneva batted away the impulse to toss her towel at Stephanie Binks. She started to turn away and then turned back to the agent and said, "I know about the fake Instagram. Did it help to sell copies?"

Stephanie Binks put her hands behind her head. Under the skylight her dark hair was lightened with gray streaks, like bursts of electricity.

Geneva went on. "I'm not being judgmental. It was clever. I assume it helped with sales and created excitement. Mira was reluctant to do anything like that for herself?"

Stephanie glanced first at Geneva's kneecaps then up at her face. When she spoke again her voice was calm, measured. "She was reluctant, that's true. She never liked dealing with publicity. Even that festival—it wasn't her idea. I had to pitch the idea to her repeatedly. She agreed only as a favor to me. Maybe I should still be grateful to her. I have plenty of other clients, but she was the draw. I probably kept those clients because I worked with her, although people are forgetting that now."

"Who helped you with the social media posts? Who gave you photographs?"

"Various people. I took some of my own. I don't really care that you know. It's not a crime."

"You assumed her identity?"

"You don't really ask questions, do you? Your questions are answers. Listen, I was her agent. She needed me to market her work—and her."

"What about her mother? Did she help? Were you friends with Eileen?"

"I don't think you need to know—"

"It's interesting though, isn't it? People might think that Mira's mother was pushed into it, that someone forced her to give up photographs . . ."

"That's not the case at all. Of course not. Although it took me too long to understand how much her mother disliked her. She finally cared about her daughter in her last year—because Eileen was dying and dependent. Mira said it was like a religious conversion, how her mother changed. "

"A religious conversion. Was someone responsible for that?"

"I've always imagined it was the priest—the one Mira gave all her money to. Someone had to make Eileen realize there was more to life than spite."

"But you profited from spite. You used the photos she gave you—for Mira's social accounts."

Stephanie stretched her arms above her head, twisted from side to side, taking her time before she answered. "Eileen wouldn't have had the wit to give me anything. My god. As for Mira and her needs, you should realize I created a persona for her—someone more vivid than she was. Mira was private, awkward, better one-on-one than in groups. She had a bit of a complex, actually. She was always thinking about what other people wanted—it could be seen as controlling and manipulative. Maybe it was. My revealing her identity was good for her. I helped her get beyond herself. She had to work out her psychological problems through her books, had to kill off quite a few people. At least on Instagram she wasn't killing anyone. When representing her I always tried to think of things not only through her perspective but through the reader's. Readers need to feel connected. I helped forge those connections. You don't understand at all, do you? Do you think it stops stinging—Mira's death? You have no idea. I should have been with her—someone should have. She might have been saved. That's what stings."

The agent's face looked ravaged.

"I'm sorry," Geneva said. "It must have been terrible for you—to lose her. Especially given that it's not clear how she died, that it's still a mystery."

The agent laughed, a dry hard laugh. "It's not a mystery. People like you just want it to be a mystery. As if every human life is a story meant for your entertainment. What happened to Mira was an accident. A freak accident. You want it to be murder though, don't you? You know what that makes you? A ghastly little fiend."

Geneva took a shallow breath, exhaled. "I know that it wasn't an accident, Stephanie. You can't try to convince me otherwise."

"Who's trying?" Stephanie Binks said.

↦ CHAPTER TWENTY-ONE

S HE SHOULD GO HOME, Geneva told herself. And yet. Something in Stephanie Binks's manner confused her. Was the agent playing with Geneva's emotions only to see how she reacted? Geneva hadn't thought so when she was in the agent's presence. Now she wondered.

She didn't open the text that came in from Thom, didn't want to deal with him—not yet. She didn't want to hear him explain himself again.

She changed out of her swimsuit in her room and was heading down to the lobby to grab a coffee from the mobile café when she was stopped.

"Did you forget me?" Yolanda Eng grasped Geneva's elbow. "Aren't you supposed to do a real interview with me? Didn't we talk about arranging that? I have lots to say, okay? To you and your co-editor."

Before Geneva could respond, Yolanda said, "Or never mind about your partner. I think I'd like to talk to you alone anyway. We had a real adventure in the woods, didn't we? I felt for sure we'd find Tama, but somebody else beat us to it."

Yolanda chose a padded armchair in the main lounge area in sight of the elevators. She clutched a tote bag on her lap and stroked the fabric.

"Is that—?" Geneva asked.

"Yes! I had it made on Etsy. It's my favorite photo of the two of us." The faces on the tote bag were unmistakable: Mira and Yolanda, young, long-haired, shining teeth. Behind them, a backdrop that suggested dying trees in a half-burned forest.

Yolanda chuckled. "It's so funny to see Thom Kleist again. He calls himself Thom Crystl, but I'll always know him as Thom Kleist, Father Kleist. Funny that you're editing a book about Mira, or is it turning into a full-scale biography, given all the material you must be gathering?" She chuckled again, shaking her head, like someone amazed by a funny joke. "It's wild that Mira put Thom in her will. She was in love with him, I'm betting. Big age difference. It didn't matter. She must have relished overcoming a stumbling block. I can say that about Mira—she was competitive, and I know that because I knew Mira better than anyone. Better than Thom certainly. Thom wouldn't have known her for many years—after he scooted away or socked himself away or whatever people like that do when they turn into priests. You can't imagine what she was like years ago—always secretive, always ashamed of herself. And competitive. And then moving away and then—when people found out she wrote the novels it didn't take a Freudian."

Geneva lowered her voice, hoping Yolanda would do the same, and asked, "What do you mean?"

Yolanda patted her tote bag until the faces wrinkled. "All that repression, that fear of disapproval. She must have wanted to be a good girl for too long. So in those novels she popped out of her shell and showed herself as not such a good girl after all. And then she says to hell with it and starts doing those photo shoots and posting things online. Terrible that she died. You'd think a single woman would have more resources."

"I still don't understand," Geneva said.

"Good god. She wanted the Kleist brothers' attention—wanted them to save her soul."

"Are you sure you understood what she wanted?"

"I was her friend. Her only real friend. I gave her clarity. A reminder of where she came from. I inspired her—my energy inspired her."

Geneva was thinking that maybe it's a disease writers like Mira have to endure: everyone they meet believes they're an inspiration.

"Think of it," Yolanda went on. "She took away Thom's father from the family, didn't she? God knows what he tried to do to her when she gave him a shove, right? That's what had to have happened. She was very pretty. She goes downstairs. Thom's father goes after her on the stairs. Next thing you know he's the one taking a tumble."

"She told you this?"

"It doesn't take a genius to put two and two together. She not only took away Thom's father, her own mother took away his mother. It was all about attraction—how much time those women spent together. Terri Kleist was infatuated with Eileen Wallacz— you couldn't keep her away from Eileen. Those Kleist boys never really stood a chance. Not much of a home life. Boys don't thrive on neglect."

Three women passed by slowly, not hiding that they were trying to listen. Yolanda leaned in, nearly resting her head on Geneva's shoulder. "I'm sorry—I just—I had vodka in my room. The fact is, I miss Mira. I wasn't myself for a long time after she passed. There was so much she could have done, if she had allowed herself. The thing I didn't understand was why she left the festival. Mira hated nature. Ticks—she didn't want to get a tick bite or to run into Oakley Beals. He was always out hiking or saying he was hiking. A creep. Have you seen the portrait he did of her? It's like a confession. Those stones he put around Mira's head."

"They're supposed to be steps."

Yolanda leaned back. "Steps? Those aren't steps. My god. Steps! He'd like to have taken some steps, let me tell you. He was old enough to be Mira's father, but he had the biggest crush on her. He kept trying to get her away from her own mother. For what reason? Her mother needed her, depended on her in the final days—and Mira liked being needed. Or looking like she was needed. She had to be writing all day and into the night for most of her adult life. I can't imagine she was that much of a help to her mother before her mother's health began failing. A very sweet woman, Eileen. Sweet to me and to a lot of people. She had trouble with Mira, that's true, because Mira could be exasperating, acting above herself, above all of us. Mira had a way of making even her own mother uneasy. Oakley Beals despised Eileen because she wouldn't let him come worming around the house to see Mira. If Mira was murdered—I'm not saying she was—I used to think it had to be Oakley Beals. Ten years ago he practically lived in those woods. He knew where every stone was."

Geneva's head was pounding. Oakley Beals. Had her speculations about his portrait revealed the truth? A possibility occurred to her—the intuition sharp enough that she drew in her breath. "You were friends with Mira for a long time," she said. "You must have a lot of photos of her."

Yolanda fondled her tote bag. "I do. If you'd like some early photos for your book I could help you out."

"Did you already help out Stephanie Binks? Giving her photos to post online?"

The air filled with invisible thistles. Everything became quiet until on the far side of the lounge laughter echoed.

Yolanda slumped in her chair, without looking at Geneva. "I wanted to be helpful," she said. "I've always been helpful. I don't think anything's wrong with being helpful."

"You must have figured out that the social media sites—there was more than one, I'm learning—weren't managed by Mira."

"Stephanie was her agent. Whatever Stephanie needed had to be for Mira's own good, for her career, you know? To get people talking about her, interested in her. Excited about her. To create stronger relationships with readers. It's all about relationships, Stephanie says. That's how you get readers. I was doing Mira a favor." Yolanda stared at her hands before she looked again at Geneva. When she spoke next, her voice was tight, her jaw stiff. "They all know each other, those women you've been interviewing. They know who you are and who Thom is. You're not tricking any of them. They're having fun, letting you play detective. They have contempt for you—and especially for Thom."

Geneva took a breath, tried to calm down as the blood rushed to her head.

"We think he did it, most of us," Yolanda went on. "He was at the conference hall, after all—but he told the police he wasn't. Probably someone should have squealed on him back then. He had the motive. And he must have wanted her to pay for what she did to his father."

"You mean about falling down the stairs—Thom's father? Even if it's true that his father harassed her she wouldn't have meant for him to die. It would have been an accident."

"Everyone has a story about that. The man hits his head going up or down the steps. I don't even remember the direction he was supposedly going anymore. Terri Kleist went around saying no one was at fault, and in the same breath letting people know who got the stairs wet. She didn't have to mention Mira at all, but she did. And then people put it together—that maybe her husband was tangling with Mira. She was always a pretty girl. Maybe there was something going on there and Mira had to protect herself—you can imagine the rest. Whatever happened, most people blamed Mira, going down there in a bathing suit. Tempting an old guy. We're not exactly the most enlightened town. Her own mother was a lovely woman, but she couldn't help but feel disappointed in Mira for being a flirt."

Geneva waited until two more women passed by and out of hearing range. "Her mother blamed her?"

Yolanda finally lowered her voice. "Whatever Terri said, Eileen believed—even against her own daughter."

"But not in the end? Eileen adored her daughter in the end."

"Well, Eileen was sick. She clung to Mira, and so Terri Kleist was left out in the cold. They were neighbors. You know that, right? Eileen and Terri were very close. Very supportive of one another. Maybe too much so. Eileen tried to be a good mother to Mira, but Mira didn't make it easy. Mira never made anything easy for anyone who cared for her."

Geneva said, "About Oakley Beals—you said he might have had something to do with Mira's murder. Do you believe he killed her?"

"He was in those woods often. Mira felt sorry for him. I suppose anyone could come to resent that. I've always thought it was a possibility that he was the culprit. Maybe he asked to meet her there. Who knows? It's been a long time since it happened. And finally it was ruled an accident, so what are you going to think? No evidence for anything. It's comical, you and Thom, trying to get people to talk. Acting innocent. If it was murder, my money's on Thom, not Oakley. But who knows? I don't understand why Thom came back to this place. But then murderers return to the scene of the crime.

Don't look at me like that! It's hard to account for what accumulated rage can do."

"You texted me that photo of Thom, right? That was you?"

Yolanda grinned. "You can thank me for that later."

⁇ CHAPTER TWENTY-TWO

THE SUN FLASHED through cloud banks, turning the woods gold and silver before dissolving the light back to gray. The wind was quiet here and leaves were thick on the ground— old leaves, slippery, some of them.

Not far ahead was the spot where Geneva experienced the shock of seeing Mira, the triumph too. The silly pride she had felt, for she was the one to find the author, no one else. The warmth of that realization and then the terror. What had made her grasp the hand of a woman who should have intimidated her too much for Geneva to imagine she could ever touch her? What led her to take such a liberty and to drag the woman after her? And yet she had known, her senses alert, her skin feathering with fear, that they were in danger. The girl she was—she wouldn't recognize her now, wouldn't understand her. And yet that girl was right.

In memory the background of her first and only encounter with Mira Wallacz was coming into focus. Her mind must have been recording more than she had been aware of. Now, after all these years, she could see what surrounded the two of them, for the wind had come up back then. The oak leaves thrashing. Above her the faint sawing of branches. The decaying smell of fallen leaves, the slushy sound of leaves under her feet in those spots where the soil was damp.

Mira might have heard the moment stones began to fall. Might have begun to run or might have slipped on leaves and stumbled.

The sound of the wind rising again and unsettling leaves—the leaves above Geneva, and then too there were many leaves clustered under her feet. So many leaves, she would hear anyone coming, crashing through. Unless they were already near.

A sensation of pressure filled her ears. The air snapped next to her head. At her feet, a scattering of pebbles. The sun was in her eyes, and for a moment whatever was in the tree above her existed as a stretched gray shadow.

"Remember me, ma'am? You were just a kid back then. I know your face."

She blinked until her vision cleared. The flicker of familiarity.

"You remember me?" the voice asked again.

She looked up. High in the tree was the man who had been hosing the steps when she left the church. And then—the jolt of an old memory, as if a hand pushed her shoulder.

"The bus?" she said. "You were on the bus a long time ago? You were tossing something in the air? That was you? Ten years ago?"

"Yup."

When she didn't say anything he repeated himself, shouting "Yup" down at her, louder this time. "It was fun," he said. "You were my first. I mean, I meant you were going to be my first. Just for fun."

The bark on the trunk of the tree appeared to shrink.

"You were only a kid," she said.

"Not anymore. Are you sorry?"

"I'm very sorry," she said. I am, she told herself. I am very, very sorry.

"Could you be my girlfriend?" His voice was a whistle.

"Sure." Her own voice was a half-whisper, half-squeak.

He laughed, a high hooting sound. "You're such a liar. You lie all the time. You like to lie. You like liars. That lady who was here back then, she was a liar."

"You mean, she lied because she wrote stories?"

"They're lies, aren't they?"

"Do you write stories?"

"I'm not a liar, liar."

She made herself look away and then up again. The man raised his hand and kept it raised, his fingers curled. If she ran he'd throw whatever he was holding. If she didn't run he would throw with better aim. She felt a weight on the side of her forehead. Stinging. She touched her head. Her hand came away wet—not blood. Something wet from the tree.

The leaves were sliding under her feet, the ground spongy. To get up from a stumble she pressed her hands against a tree's trunk. And then—leaves spinning above her. She would never be as fast as the man. Her breath caught in her throat. She heard her own breathing. She recognized she was running in the wrong direction, away from the conference center, deeper into the woods.

Her right foot sank into something as soft as flesh. Her throat closed and she couldn't scream. She pulled up her foot and stumbled forward. The sound of leaves kicking up close behind her. A terrible taste in her mouth.

A voice rang out yards ahead of her. "He wants to scare you. He'd never hurt anyone too badly anyway." A woman's voice. A pause, and then the person shouted into the air, "Get down, idiot!"

Standing before Geneva was an older person in a silver puff vest, her hands on her hips. A satchel slung over her shoulder. The woman's hair was cut very short, salt and pepper. Everything about the woman carried an air of authority.

"Sorry to call the poor guy an idiot," the woman said, "but that's the only name he'll understand. He knows all about Mira, everyone in town knows about her and about the conference—and he thought he could scare you, that's all."

With relief, Geneva nearly fell into the woman's arms. Her throat was still closed from terror.

After a long silence the woman said, "I remember you. I wanted to find you. To thank you for being friends with my son."

"That was him?" Geneva asked. "In the tree?"

The woman gasped. "God no. That was one of the local crazies. Can I say that word now—*crazies*? Hard to know what's acceptable. My son isn't impaired in any way. He never has been. Thom's your friend, isn't he? I'm glad to see you, you know that? You were the little girl who was going to be in the same room with me at the center, years ago. I just couldn't stay, couldn't abide what was going on."

Geneva began to understand. "Ten years ago—you came here, to the festival? You're Thom's mother? You're Terri Kleist?"

"You can see the resemblance to Thom?"

Geneva didn't. "Does he know you're here?"

"Oh no."

Geneva said, "He'll be so happy to see you."

"Will he? I'm never sure. I was here with Mira, right near where you're standing."

"You were here right where we're standing—in the past?" Geneva repeated. "Here?"

"Oh yes. I couldn't stop Mira from walking not far from where you are right now. Daring people. Mira never wanted to be forgiven."

Geneva stepped backward. "Why did she need to be forgiven?"

"The boys thought she killed their father. I said their father had been drinking. The truth was, my husband hadn't been drinking—not that day. Mira was always reckless. Uncontrollable even then and silly, very silly. She didn't know herself. She was going to put what happened into one of her novels and blame my boys. It was just a matter of time. I was tired of waiting for that to happen."

Geneva reached out to rest her hand on Terri Kleist's arm and then pulled back. "We have to go to the convention center," she said.

"You go."

She's old, Geneva repeated to herself silently. She's old and she's weak. She can't hurt anyone. Aloud she said, "Let's walk back to the center together. I can help you find Thom."

"No, not now." Terri Kleist turned away.

Geneva kept her voice steady. "Where are you going?"

"I'm not sure. Maybe home. I feel called back."

"I won't leave without you," Geneva said. "It's not safe for you here."

"Is that so? You think I'm afraid of that silly young man? I'm sorry he frightened you. This place was very important to me and to Mira's mother. Someone told you about that, and so that's why you're here? To be nosy? Thom didn't tell you. Thom wouldn't know what this place meant to us. He's not as observant as his brother."

"I don't think anyone should be alone here."

"You were alone."

"I know. So stupid of me."

"Stupid, maybe. We all can be stupid. Not thinking of consequences. My husband went to bed that night not knowing what that fall did to him."

"It was an accident, Thom said."

"Mira never did anything by accident. She wrote about all sorts of things. She was terrible to everyone when she wrote those things online. Wicked. Making good people into cartoons online and in her novels too. I could never confront her about it while Eileen was alive. And then, I don't know why, in the end Eileen stopped being my friend. That had to be Mira's doing. That and the stuff she wrote—that hurt us all."

"You're talking about Mira's online accounts? Accounts are hijacked. It's easily done. You must have come across something that was fake. Let's go back."

"I'm fine. You're the one who needs to go back." Terri Kleist was walking away.

Her heart racing, Geneva said, "Wait. Tell me, have you seen George lately?'

Terri Kleist turned. "The priest in town told me he's in San Diego now. I could fly there. Surprise him. He hasn't come to see me in such a long time. I wasn't sure he was still in California." She swallowed what sounded like a sob. "No, too late. Why do I say what I don't mean? The case of Mira's death will be reopened again, won't it, because of you and Thom—I heard all about what you two are trying to do. It's all they talk about up at the conference center. Thom never does what I ask, ever. With George it's like he reads my mind. He has a wonderful life. He's helped so many. So many depend on him."

She clutched her satchel. "Mira must have been lying, lying about me and about the boys to her mother. I know that's what George understood. George thinks the way I do. He always has—when it counts. He understands me and I understand him."

Geneva felt her panic rising, making her dizzy. "We should go now. Let's head back together. It's getting cold. It'll be dark soon. Let's go."

Terri Kleist's face stiffened. "I should have been the one to take care of Eileen when she was ill. She heard stories that couldn't be true."

Geneva hesitated before she said. "Maybe what you thought about Mira, maybe it wasn't true? We can talk about that, we can figure it out."

The woman's eyes darkened. "You're a very strange girl—a real piece of work. Eileen and I should have come back here again, you know that. It's a sacred place."

"There was a stream near here?" Geneva said. If she kept talking, perhaps Terri Kleist would calm down and return to the conference center with her. Or someone else would come and help them.

The branches of an oak clattered in another gust.

"I'll just go a ways farther on," Terri Kleist said, her voice softening. "You have to head back. It's not a good idea for you to be here. Be careful where you walk. There are drop offs. People don't always see the cliff face until they nearly tumble. You shouldn't be here. Mira shouldn't have been here either. It wasn't her place. She stepped into it all right. George wouldn't have liked that. Not at all. Not George."

Geneva reached out to take Terri Kleist's hand. The woman flinched, patted her satchel. "Everything is explained right in here, okay? But I want you to remember what I'm telling you, all right?"

She stared hard into Geneva's eyes again. "I didn't mean for it to happen. It was just that it was our place, Eileen's and mine. We went here when we were girls, Eileen and I. And later too. For years. It was our secret. No one was to know. I wanted the place to reject anyone else. I didn't like what Mira did to her mother and me in those novels. I didn't hate her—she just needed to be corrected. People need that. I didn't mean for it to happen. She moved all of a sudden and stepped right in front and bent down—she didn't have to do that. Do you remember everything I just said? You're here to find out who killed Mira. Every one of those people"—she tilted her head toward the direction of the conference center—"every single one of them knows what you're up to. The truth has to come out. I'm confessing to you. I was the one. No one else. Mira stepped right where she shouldn't have stepped. Remember what I'm telling you. There's a note in my satchel and another one I left at the center. Remember. Are you ever ashamed of yourself and angry? Maybe it's not wrong to be angry, just wrong not to do anything about it. This was a sacred place—what Eileen and I had together. It's not for anybody else. I don't know why you thought you could come here."

Thom's mother was stepping away, pushing forward.

When Geneva heard something behind her she turned. Later she would wonder if she imagined it—the change in temperature, the air opening and closing, like a door shutting beside her.

And then, unmistakable, not far ahead: a sound like a branch cracking and falling, although it wasn't a branch.

⤕ CHAPTER TWENTY-THREE

T HE DETECTIVE was struck by the coincidence—that Geneva Finch was the last to see two women directly before their deaths—in the same wooded area. What were the chances?

Geneva could only recount what Terri Kleist had told her. That she didn't mean to harm Mira Wallacz. A suppressed laugh from one of the policemen, young, with a bluish growth of beard that gave him a cadaverous appearance. "She had awfully good aim," he said.

Terri Kleist's speech was confused. But the notes she left behind were clear: she confessed to killing Mira Wallacz. Terri Kleist only meant to frighten Mira. And then Terri's guilt had eaten her alive and she ended her own life.

For Thom, the loss of his mother—an incalculable loss. A mother who chooses to stop living—no words for such a loss.

It wouldn't be unnatural for Geneva to feel she hadn't done enough, hadn't stopped Thom's mother from killing herself. Had not stopped a death—twice.

One of the officers took pity on Geneva. He looked down at her and said, in a half-whisper that made her heart clutch, "Don't be guilty. There's no logical explanation for a suicide."

Nights were worst for Geneva. She was again in the woods, again hearing the last sound Terri Kleist heard.

Often Aida repeated to Geneva, "You didn't do anything wrong. That woman was determined."

It would be months before Geneva could begin to see herself apart from what happened. She met with a therapist and tried to forgive herself. Eventually, Geneva let Aida and Elson attempt to help her. The three of them went to the new restaurant, The Casebook, to listen to their favorite client interpret Frank Sinatra. Charlie was an excellent Sinatra, but they all knew his act couldn't last forever. What does? Even certain kinds of sadness—they return but may, with time, begin to dim.

Charlie continued to bring magazines to the office for Geneva. One day in April she came across a new poem by Thom Crystl in *The Atlantic*. A poem about the clarity of air, and small flowers, and how you could never forget such beauty—the beauty of a city in Switzerland.

Weeks later she came across another poem by Thom Crystl, and this time the poem was online in a small journal: "Featherless Hope." About a hotel room, hearing the couple on the other side of the wall. The poem was nearly a direct transcript of what Thom Crystl told her that night after the party as she was driving him to his hotel.

She reread the poem, thinking the tone sounded angry. And maybe the poem was angry. She considered another possibility. That the poet wanted her to know he remembered that night with her.

The high heels Charlie brought to the office for her—his wife's castoffs—weren't quite as outrageously high as usual. Beautiful, deep black with a loose ankle strap.

"If those don't give you confidence," Charlie said, "I don't know what will."

"You think I'm not confident?" She smiled at him, grateful to be able to tease him the way she used to.

Charlie's grin scattered light in his eyes. "Life comes at you hard, my father used to tell me. And he's dead, so he knew what he was talking about. But look at you. You'll be practically strutting in no time."

At her desk across the office, Aida echoed Charlie. Geneva had to be coming back to herself. It was past time.

"By the way, I ran into George," Charlie said. "He was looking for you."

Geneva shivered.

Charlie went on, "That band of his is hanging on. People never tire of that crap."

Her heart quieted. Charlie meant George Harrison in the tribute band. Not Terri Kleist's oldest son.

After Charlie left and they were alone again in the office, Aida prodded. "You should arrange to see Thom Crystl. Unfinished business. Really. He adores you—that's what I think. You want to hear something funny? He always reminded me of someone, and now I know who it is."

Geneva waited.

"You. He reminds me of you, Geneva. The ways he talks and moves. It's like he knows you at some deep, strange level. Like what they say about compatible couples. They have similar rhythms." She laughed. "Either that or he's impersonating you."

One Sunday afternoon Geneva sat down determined to read Mira Wallacz's posthumously published novel. The uncanny premise: a woman struck by falling rocks dies. Geneva knew much of the plot already from spoiler reviews. The coincidence between the plot and the facts of Mira's death sickened her. Nevertheless, finally she was ready, ready again to hear her favorite author's voice.

She hadn't finished the first chapter before her skin quivered into alertness.

Mira would never put "said" before every proper name. Never something as simple but awkward as "said Elena" reiterated continually, with long explanations about the character's tone of voice. Never allow a logjam of adjectives to turn her sentences turgid. Never invest such clinical detail in a sex scene.

Maybe an overly zealous editor went to work on the writing? Geneva read the next chapter and the next. The prose was jammed with bad choices. Not Mira's. She was sure of it: the posthumous novel wasn't written by Mira.

Thom should be told, shouldn't he? She had answered his earlier emails with condolences and apologies. For the first time she answered him at length, telling him about her life, hoping he would want to see her, not mentioning her suspicions about the novel.

He answered within an hour. A week later he would be in Wyandotte for a reading. Could they meet? "Don't bother coming to the reading," he wrote. "Life is short. But afterwards let's talk. I miss you." He gave her his hotel's address.

The night of the reading, once she arrived in the auditorium, she felt so self-conscious she nearly turned around and headed back to her apartment. She realized that the Dolly Parton heels Charlie dropped off at the office might telegraph she was trying too hard—the thin strip of black at the ankle, a spiked heel like the stem of a martini glass. Maybe they could pass as "whimsical," not desperate.

She sat at the back of the auditorium. A stout man with a crooked bow tie unctuously introduced Thom for far too long. And then there he was, Thom Crystl, approaching the podium: the same vulnerable eyes, hair jagged and floppy from a bad haircut. The white sleeves of his shirt rolled up, one sleeve higher than the other. He took a quick drink from the water glass on the podium, looked over the rim at the audience, set the glass down, smiled. He really was a very good-looking man.

She watched his gaze traveling the audience. Was he trying to spot her even though he advised her not to come for his reading? She leaned back into shadow.

After the reading he signed books. She waited in the corridor until the line was thinning before heading for his hotel. She didn't want to arrive before him and waited in her car until he texted with the room number.

Thom Crystl hugged her as soon as she came through the door. She pulled back, feeling anxious and shy. His suite was enormous. A bouquet of roses, pink and yellow, stood on a low table, and there was a kitchenette with a full-size refrigerator.

"It was a great reading," she said, and meant it.

"Was it? I tried. You were there? You should have let me know. I have vodka and orange juice. The basics."

While he prepared drinks in the kitchenette she stepped into the suite's living area.

On the coffee table lay a sheet of paper. Prolific Thom. She felt a wave of tenderness toward him and leaned over to read the typescript.

CHAPTER TWENTY-THREE

The sky filled with crows
crows and crows and crows and crows in crows,
rows of them
all around her. Goodness, hers.

What had Oakley Beals said about good people? That people who believe themselves to be good do dangerous things. But some people are good, naturally good.

She hadn't heard Thom enter when he returned to the room. He lifted her coat from the arm of the couch where she had placed it, opened the closet door, hung it for her. Approaching her he nearly tripped between the coffee table and the couch.

A realization: he'd been drinking. The slight swaying she had dismissed at the poetry reading as his body responding to his poems' rhythms. His over articulation. The way at one point he threw his head back, laughing at nothing.

He was in mourning, and he wasn't well.

He handed her a glass. His own was already half empty. That must have been what caused him to take so long in the other room.

Now she wasn't sure if she should tell him that the last novel published under Mira's name wasn't written by Mira. The novel had been wildly successful. The author's death, the echoes of the novel's content, had proved a lure. An ugly lure. Amazing no one else had pointed out the subterfuge. Tama Squires, the biographer, had become a casual friend and had told her something was strange about that last novel—maybe she had come closest to wondering about the style in which it was written. Because of her injury the biographer hadn't been writing as much, was still devoting herself to her recovery.

Geneva thought she could tell Thom what she suspected, tell him and leave. He deserved to know—unless, it occurred to her, he already knew.

"Did someone else write Mira's last novel? I read it—at last. Thom, she didn't write it."

He tilted his head. He hadn't heard her, apparently.

She repeated herself.

Thom Crystl choked back a laugh and said, "Who could write like Mira? Are you playing games?"

Her face heated. "Games? I never play games. Was someone hired to write it for the royalties and to increase interest? Whoever wrote it made sure that the plot was about Mira's death. That guaranteed interest. Maybe you didn't know that someone else wrote the novel?"

When he didn't answer her, she waited. He finished what was left in his glass. Stood before her, shifting from foot to foot. Nearly a full minute passed in silence.

At last she said, "I can't stay, Thom. I guess I have my answer."

His face fell with disappointment and more, something close to anger.

"You like that—to leave," he said. "You talked with my mother, didn't you? You filled her head with ideas."

Geneva was so confused she couldn't speak. Finally, she said, "Thom, before I saw your mother in the woods I never had more than a minute's conversation with her. I was put in the same room with her all those years ago. We didn't hardly—talk—then."

"I don't believe that."

The air glinted with sparks. Go back to the beginning, Geneva told herself, retrace your steps. She quieted her breathing and asked, "Did you mean to find me at the party, when we first met?"

"A coincidence. Weird but a coincidence. Unless it wasn't a co-incidence for you. So many coincidences."

To her left, a mirror, a light switch.

He took an unsteady step toward her. "Was it a game?" he said. "All of it? You wanted my confession? Was it a game to get me to tell you what you already thought you knew?"

"Nothing has been a game for me—nothing that we did," she said. "Was it a game for you? You really didn't believe in what we were doing? Not ever?"

If it was a game that meant he had come to the conference to watch her, a game where he knew all the rules. Or he came with her to make sure she didn't find out the truth. She couldn't say what she wanted to say: I work with impersonators. They become someone else to survive. Who did you become?

The door was behind him. Her tongue felt large in her mouth. She didn't have to ask his permission to leave.

He was laughing. "Your face," he said, bitterly. "You saw me that day with Mira? Is that right? You strung me along. You thought you saw me and told my mother you saw me? Is that true? You were only playing a part because you knew what happened to Mira, and you thought you saw me there? You told my mother you saw me with Mira and she made up a confession so everyone would think she—? You played a part?"

These were only questions, Geneva told herself. A question is often an answer. Someone told her that. Who was it?

She echoed Thom's words. "I played a part?" Did he mean that he was there in the woods years ago when she'd been with Mira, that it was his presence she felt when she clutched Mira's hand?

She turned to the side to slide past him.

He clutched her arm. "Be careful. Watch where you step. You don't want to hit your head or take a fall. You'll slip on a stair if you're not careful. There's someone who would hurt you. I know there is. Someone who wants you to believe anything. You did see me, didn't you when Mira—?" He couldn't finish the sentence.

She would think about what he said later, put everything he was saying together. He was drunk and didn't know what he was telling her. Or he did know? And to escape him she had to give the impression everything was fine, that he hadn't said anything to make her fear for her life. Play dumb, play dead. Play your part.

"Thom, I should be going. Aida's waiting for me." Her voice sounded calm to her own ears.

She took a step again toward the door. Her coat was still in the closet. She would have to leave without it, could not risk spending a moment more with Thom Crystl.

"Don't go," he said. "Don't go without telling me the truth. You saw what happened with Mira. Tell me what you saw."

He raised his hands to his face, wiped at the flesh there. Brought his hands down to his side.

"Thom—you're not well."

"Who deserves to be well? You knew everything!"

She could predict what would happen next—the air fine-grained, his hands pushing her backwards until she was stumbling, her head bashed against the coffee table. His preferred mode: a head wound. So simple: people fall, rocks fall, a tree branch falls.

He was drunk, maybe too drunk.

He was a murderer. He had already murdered.

He staggered and nearly stumbled against the couch. She felt herself sliding away from him, her left heel slipping off, her right arm straining to break her fall. She jerked forward as the edge of the end table came into her peripheral vision. She was on the floor, crouching. His face was coming close to hers, blotting out everything around her. She turned her head and her cheek scraped against carpeting.

She was pinned by his weight. Her fingers were slippery and what they curled around slid from her grasp. She reached again, pulled herself forward, and caught at what her fingers kept missing. She thrust the heel against Thom Crystl's neck, thrust and twisted until, gasping, choking, he rolled away from her.

↠ CHAPTER TWENTY-FOUR

TAMA

T HINK OF IT: priest, con-man, poet. Certainly the whole story has to be of interest to Netflix. I suppose he's on suicide watch. I've never dealt much with criminals before, but you always need a new string on your bow.

So many women fall in love with prisoners. Because presumably the fellow can't harm you while he's incarcerated. A big plus.

Should I have sympathy for him—seeing him shackled? Will he be shackled? Will he appear pathetic, lonely? Is he going to pretend he's innocent again? I can ask him all sorts of questions, and he can't do a thing about it. What's he going to do? Kill me? He's in prison for what amounts to life. Thanks to his lawyers.

Those chaps were more focused on making names for themselves than in defending Thom Crystl. Well, who could defend him? His brother? At the trial George Kleist looked so much like Thom that it was disorienting. Other than his appearance, he's not at all like Thom, who lacks his older brother's clarity, his certainty. Thom, a very messy-minded fellow. George, a highly competent personality, and clearly ashamed of Thom, an attitude that, I have to admit, didn't seem appropriate in a priest.

Well, I have reasons to be resentful. George Kleist isn't even allowing me an interview. You'd think he would want his brother's story to be rounded out, which is what I'm best at—rounding out stories, giving dimensionality to lives.

Will I have to sit at a table and talk to Thom Crystl over the phone while he stares ominously at me through smudged glass? Or am I thinking of scenes that only occur in movies? I guess he'll be in one of those ugly jump suits. That suits him. He's a murderer and he used to be a priest so god knows he's accustomed to wearing what amounts to a uniform. And he's a poet. He should come by poverty honestly.

Of course now poor Geneva Finch thinks that maybe there's more to Thom Crystl's story. I keep repeating to her, Listen you're the one who poked a hole in his throat, dearie, not me. I suppose she has a story to tell which might add another level to any account I come up with. She says she jumped to conclusions—he was in mourning, drunk, unstable. She claims he had no motive. I keep telling her the truth: he did have a motive: revenge. Mira Wallacz very likely killed his father—pushed the old man when he got grabby on the stairs. Thom knew because Mira, I'd bet anything, confessed to him. As a priest he was used to confessions, just not one like hers, about the cause of his own father's death.

Poor, naïve Geneva—she thinks she can uproot the "real killer." She keeps telling me to look into this Oakley Beals character, a portrait painter. No motive, I tell her. What about Thom's brother, George? He believed Thom was guilty and didn't want to implicate his brother even more than what was already established, that was obvious. Geneva says maybe George was there at the conference center and Thom made up the story about how George was officiating at the Mass for him. He claimed as much to protect George—who was the real killer. And the photo of Thom—maybe that was of George? What about that? They're dead ringers for each other. Geneva kept asking about that photo. Now you're really losing me, I let her know. I continue to remind her: Thom confessed that George was at the Mass, filling in for him, remember? Mass takes time—I know that from Lizette's complaints as a former Catholic schoolgirl who shoplifted regularly while she was supposed to be attending services. A Mass can be shortened, Geneva says—and who would notice? Too complicated, I tell her. Life is never that complicated. Plus, no motive. What about anger? Geneva says. Rage at Mira—if she confessed to George, not Thom, that his father died because of her? George Kleist is an actual priest, I tell her, not one of those defrocked priests, like poor murderous Thom Crystl. Priests are trained to repress their emotions.

Mira just won't let it go. What if Thom's covering for his brother? Geneva keeps asking. No, I tell her. No one does that for a sibling. Sibling rivalry. Cain? Abel? Or, Geneva asks, what if Terri Kleist confessed because she thought George killed Mira? Terri Kleist believed Thom was at Mass, after all. That's what Thom told the authorities, and his mother had no reason to believe otherwise. She made a false confession to cover for her older son, George, undoubtedly her favorite child. So now Geneva thinks Terri Kleist wanted to protect George. That still wouldn't exonerate Thom as the murderer.

And what about Mira's agent? Geneva asks. What about her? She's rotten, Geneva says. Rot, I try to convince her, is not evidence. Besides—as if Stephanie Binks would stoop so low. She's more sophisticated than that. She's brilliant at what she does. She's manipulative, yes, but that's what any writer wants in an agent—someone who will change reality. In fact, Stephanie's offered to represent my next book. Feeling profoundly fortunate!

So what can I do for poor Geneva? And then I realize I can do something for her after all.

We're having lunch at this place on 25th St. and Geneva is looking downcast, as usual. I lean over my plate and say, "You asked me—twice—why Mira was in the woods when you found her there."

"I didn't think you'd ever tell me," she says.

"I thought you'd guess. It's so obvious."

I can't stop myself from making her wait, and then I give in: "Mira was there to spread her mother's ashes."

Geneva looks past my shoulder as if she sees a ghost. I turn around. No one is approaching, not even the waiter.

I go on, "Her mother died three months earlier than when you saw Mira in the woods. Her mother had a spot near there that she always liked. Kind of a little valley with the ground rising on each side. Mira probably was climbing up to spread her mother's ashes and unsettled the rocks when she climbed down."

"Did the investigators know this?"

"Not then and not now, to my knowledge. I don't see how that information could be useful this late in the game."

So there we are, having a nice lunch, and Geneva puts her hand over her heart. I'm immediately embarrassed. Please don't sob, I want to beg her.

"It was all there in writing?" she says, in a stunned voice. "Mira promised her mother in a letter that she would honor a wish to spread her ashes there—in that place?"

I'm tempted to brush Geneva's hair out of her eyes. I clarify what I know: "Her mother probably made the request in person at the end of her life—but the portion about the place she loved in those woods—that was in a long letter. Why would Mira be in the woods for so long other than to visit the place her mother loved? And to scatter her mother's ashes. It doesn't matter though, does it? Someday I should take a walk into those woods to find the exact spot, except that idea gives me the shivers. I'm not sure how much on-site research I ever want to do."

Geneva is talking too fast. "That's why she wanted Thom with her," she says, lowering her voice to a whisper. "She visited that lodge she was thinking of buying and then waited for him in town. Because he was confused about the time and the place they were to meet he came to the conference center instead. He didn't know why she wanted him to meet her. When he didn't arrive for the lunch appointment in town she set off on her own, deep into those woods. She believed in him—as a spiritual adviser and friend. He'd attended to her and her mother as her mother was dying. She wanted him with her when she spread her mother's ashes. Her trust in him, by then, was complete."

I hate to watch poor Geneva trying to untwist the events of that day so long ago. I tell her, "Well, maybe she did or maybe she didn't. He shouldn't have killed her, whatever she believed."

Geneva is half-rising out of her chair. So excited she's nearly levitating. "He didn't kill her. Tama, believe me, please, I know he didn't. Someone else did. I'll find out who. I think I have an idea. Already. It's always about the one with the quirkiest motive in Mira's novels. That's where I'll look. I won't give up. It's someone who knew exactly where she was—that's who's guilty. Someone who knew about the ashes."

"What? You're going to every crematorium and check on who knew about the ashes?"

Geneva doesn't finish her lunch but sits there, conniving, fabulating. I clean out the rest of her bento box for her. Except for the fake sushi.

Really. I can't help myself. Being with Geneva, it's like something out of *Silas Marner*—which I read for my ninth grade English class back in the old days. Hated the book, but I've never forgotten what George Eliot has the weaver say about the toddler he took in and won't give up: "she's a lone thing and I'm a lone thing." Maybe that's a paraphrase, but close enough.

"So who is it?" I ask, "who's the real murderer, if it's not the man who tried to kill you?"

She won't say—her revenge, I guess, for my withholding the obvious both times she asked. I put it straight to Geneva, "You might as well admit you're wrong. You've been wrong enough, I guess you might as well enjoy it when you find out you were right earlier when you knew he was a murderer. You weren't wrong then. You're wrong now."

"I'm not ashamed for making a mistake about him. I'm through with that—being ashamed."

"Is that even possible?"

Before we leave the restaurant I say, "Even if you found out that some person knew Mira was in the woods to spread her mother's ashes that wouldn't mean they were guilty of killing her."

"It would be a start," Geneva says. "And I won't stop trying—"

"Oh you won't, will you? Really. It's evident you've read far too many of Mira's novels."

YOLANDA

At first it must have looked like a bad run-in with a prostitute—the high heel in the throat. Don't ask me why, but an indiscretion by a former priest seems worse than an indiscretion by an acting priest. And then, the terrible realization: his murder of my dear beloved friend Mira, and then his mother's suicide, her false confession to protect him—all of which means that he indirectly caused his own mother's self-murder. Imagine it: because he didn't admit to killing Mira he caused his own mother to die rather than implicate himself. Evil. And next he tried to kill the incredibly stupid young woman who befriended him.

I had been hoping for the death penalty.

My brother works in Newark, and I'll be helping him do the clean-out of Terri Kleist's house. There's bound to be something of interest—love letters between Terri and Eileen, ticket stubs from when Terri took Eileen and Mira to *Godspell* (I was there!), all the sort of junk that's left behind and that is saleable if it relates to Mira. I know just who to sell anything to, by the way.

Trying to be useful and to quell my own grief I've started a tribute Instagram for Mira. There are so many photographs I have of her. So many of the two of us. I'm crying. Don't mind me.

Tama, dear, the interview isn't over, is it?

INGER

The odd thing: at the end of her life Mira finally learned to write! Critics were appalled by that posthumously published novel, yet readers agree with me: it's the best thing she ever managed to put out. It's been reissued and no doubt will go into more editions. With more translations in countries no one ever knew existed. Next, a knock-off diary entry is forthcoming. Mira is now more real to people than she ever was while alive and more real than when she was dead because she's now, for sure, a dead murdered novelist. It's like everything about her writing was a clue regarding her eventual horrific demise. A deceased romantic. Not Sylvia Plath, yet echoes of Plath in terms of suicide: the suicide of Thom Crystl's mother, a woman trying to cover up her son's hideous crime. Therefore you have suicide in the mix and don't forget the near murder of Geneva Finch and the actual murder of Mira Wallacz. The whole story is death-drenched.

I don't remember who said it, that good people can't write good books. I'm not sure about that—though maybe Mira became less good at the end of her life and that less-than-goodness made her a better writer. Hard to know. Amazing, though, like her ghost rose up again and temporarily inhabited the body of Geneva Finch who grabbed a high heel and stuck it into the throat of a man twice her size and managed as a consequence to stop his next murder—of herself. Thus, Mira's murderer was discovered in a plot twist like something from any number of her unbelievable novels.

Life really is stranger than even the strangest fiction. Unfathomable.

That liar Tama—pretending to *The New York Post* that she couldn't be entirely certain if she actually did knock herself out at the conference. Her own forehead broke the branch. How do I know? After her wife left her we had a little talk about Tama. How Tama was so bullet-headed she snapped off a branch with her own skull. Tama is so vain, never wearing her glasses. She walked into walls. And into windows. And mirrors. Lizette and I laughed about that. Horrible, I know. But Tama's pretty much completely recovered and trying to work up a new project focused on Mira once again. Such a bloodhound. You have to hand it to her though. Not everything is a crime. Sometimes just an opportunity.

STEPHANIE

If that kid doesn't stop dog paddling in my lane I'll make sure he dog paddles right into a wall. The water temperature—just the way I like it. Body temperature.

When I get back to my apartment I'll lift up the good luck tokens on my dresser and thank them. I'll polish the little duck sculpture. Lovingly. Inside crouches another tiny duck. The hidden duck. Secrets inside secrets. Talismans. They always bring me luck.

The woods by the conference center, so much of that area is a thin crust. I've heard the whole state is pocked by landfills. Right under your feet run rivers of trash, ready to shift and slowly collapse and draw you in. There's a cliff not far from where Mira was wandering that day, near the slope at the end of the tree line. Being optimistic I expected a rockfall and a gentle shove would be all it would take, but then who shows up other than that girl, Geneva Finch, and the next thing I knew she was hauling Mira away like a sack of potatoes and Mira was letting her. When I saw that girl I imagined she would be blamed. Or should be. That ungainly slip of a human being. And dressed like a vagrant.

Of course I knew Mira would be in the woods, knew that first she planned to be venturing around in town the day earlier and looking into property, maybe thinking about buying a retreat house. She let me know she was considering giving up writing altogether and devoting herself to helping other writers. A really idiotic idea—making waffles and dealing with the sort of people who are the most egocentric and unsatisfied and privileged on the planet. She was going to stop in the woods for what she said was a "ritual." And then she told me about the ashes. How she hadn't collected them from the crematorium, how she would be forever grateful if I would pick them up for her. How she had been afraid of picking them up too soon after her mother's death. No, she'd flown to Seattle and abandoned her own mother's ashes at the funeral home in Bingle, that blasted town. She about lost her mind—couldn't believe her mother was dead for over two and a half months. How bizarre. Normally she would never let anyone pick up her dry cleaning let alone something like her mother's ashes. Maybe that's what put me over—the ashes.

She was going to take them into the woods and, you know, throw them around. She planned it all. She wanted me to put the ashes in a bag for her. Get them out of the urn from the funeral director's in Bingle—any urn would frighten her—and put them in a nice silk makeup bag and put multiple big baggies over the bag. I could have killed her for making that request alone. She thought her hands would shake and she'd spill her own mother's ashes . . .

The unimaginable gutless prissiness. You're going to shake the ashes out anyway, so what if some of the flakes fly around before they get where you want them to go? That's what I should have said. Like any sane person I was tempted to toss out the ashes and substitute kitty litter and gravel. She trusted me, she said, to have steady hands and pick up the ashes and hand them over to her at the conference. So that's what happened. I got those godawful ashes and put them in another bag for her and then triple bagged them. In other words, I bagged her dead mother. For that alone she deserved what she got.

Anyway, back at the time when she was in the woods wandering, I reasoned that Mira is so clumsy, she'll fall easily and knock herself out on a stone outcropping, given half a chance. No balance. One of her legs shorter than the other, like Jackie Onassis's.

But no, after she shooed off the girl she turned back. She was below the slope, cleaning out her purse, shaking her silk makeup bag, crying. She looked up. The light was still high enough to strike her eyes. And that's when I let the first rock go.

What I did—maybe I did it for the wrong reasons. Of course I believed I was rightly her executor and had no idea she changed her will. I believed I inherited her drafts and journals and all sorts of possibilities that were owed to me after creating her readership. So, yes, Mira had a big surprise for me. But I wasn't done with surprises. And I had plans for the posthumous novel just about ready to go.

This still makes me laugh: I wrapped two stones I picked up on the slope in my own sports bra so my fingerprints weren't on them. I knew better than to walk around looking suspicious by taking gloves on a jog.

And then later—ten years later, to the week—when questions began again it took so little to seal all the flaps on the incident. Even though hideous Geneva Finch and Thom were at it, stirring everyone up.

Good luck: seeing Terri Kleist at the conference, informing Terri I knew about her son, that I'd seen one of her sons in the woods, seen what he did to Mira ... Of course I knew all about those Kleist brothers. Mira used to talk about them too often, worry about them. Boring. Did Thom think I didn't immediately recognize who he was, trying to interview me when he and Geneva Finch wanted to set a trap? Well, who can set the best trap? Terri Kleist thought the world of me, was grateful I talked with her, grateful I was keeping the secret about George, her beloved boy, her darling. She never suspected Thom, whom she believed to be serving Mass that day.

After Terri Kleist couldn't help but believe her son George was a murderer she made that false confession and did a number on herself—her choice! Some people are so addled they do the world a favor by exiting a little early for all our sakes.

And then when I visited out-of-his mind drunk, grief-addled Thom Crystl, I told him the same thing I told his mother, how she confessed to me that one of her sons had been there in the woods. George was the one with the temper. Always howling when he and

Thom were kids, always furious at their drunken father, always getting into shoving matches. It couldn't be George—George was at the church, Thom said, George couldn't do it. Then who did?

His mother's death blew a hole right through Thom. Right through his mind. He knew his mother didn't harm Mira, that she wasn't capable of it. So what was there to be done? Plant the seed and he'll convince himself he's guilty—for something. And he'll never do anything to compromise George. He has an imagination. In time he'll imagine himself into whatever he hears. Someone saw you there, I told him. Maybe you came down the slope and unsettled the stones and maybe you picked one up and hadn't seen who was on the path or off the path or . . .

I told him that Geneva Finch knew he was playing a trick. She was testing him, and that's why she set up those interviews. Don't you realize she was playing a part, Thom? Didn't you see that she only wanted to trick you? It was all a game, Thom. She thinks you're guilty. Couldn't you tell when you were with her—didn't you realize?

After all, he was at the conference center years ago and lied about it to the police. I saw him there. I knew he lied. Liars keep lying. He lived an adult life, which meant there are plenty of things for which he could be guilty. Guilt, the strongest hallucinogenic. Give it time, I told myself. Give it time. And it did take time.

He might not have been certain about what happened to Mira, but he came to believe one thing: Geneva Finch was convinced of his guilt. And their interviews were her way to find out more about him. From the start she believed he was guilty and wanted him to confess.

She was the proof. She was the evidence.

Geneva Finch. It was obvious she was adept at jumping to conclusions. Nice touch—that high heel. Femme fatale in the old movie
star manner. I laughed out loud when I read the news report.

All it takes is trust—trust in the wrong person. Mira was intend-
ing to fire me, to seek representation elsewhere. I hadn't known
that before she died. I hadn't known I had a better motive.

The pool is emptying out. Just me and that ugly little frog of a kid.
God knows where his parents are. Irresponsible people, they're ev-
erywhere.

Go get 'em, tiger, my father used to say. The world is yours—
except for a long time it wasn't. You're getting too big for your
britches, my mother used to say. She thought I'd get bigger britches.
I don't wear godawful britches. Success is about being first, the first
to head off eruptions from the past. Be first and be obvious while
no one wants to believe the truth could be so simple. The truth is,
Mira made what happened to her inevitable when she stopped taking advice from me. That's not a crime if the advice is bad. But if
the advice is excellent—then it's a crime against nature.

There are other sorts of crimes—psychic crimes. Did Mira actually think I didn't recognize that the first woman killed in five of her
novels was me? Each time: I was the victim. She never explained or
apologized. Novel after novel, I kept dying.

It's not an exaggeration to say I have thrived on resentment.
Many of us do. Let no one tell you otherwise. Resentment depends
on secrecy—glamor, drama. And if the object of resentment is obliterated, another must fill that empty space. It's not so different
from love, that wish to fill emptiness—the way a widow must feel, a
widow going out on her first date after the funeral. Does that make
sense? I'm not sure it does. How could it make sense to anyone else?

CHAPTER TWENTY-FOUR

Probably Mira would have found a way to make sense of what I'm saying.

Sometimes I wonder if I'm short-changing myself. But everything's closed up now, sutured. I'll always be fine as long as I can talk to myself. I'm my own best listener.

And who even guesses the truth? And if they ever guessed what could they prove? Geneva Finch—I admit that I think about her too much. She must have always wanted Mira's death to be murder, and it was.

My backstroke really has improved.

That kid who nearly kicked me in the face as he splashed on by . . . If he knocks his skull hard against the wall it will be his own fault. I don't need to see that—how delicate, how vulnerable the skull is. Life will teach him.

LUISA

I was outside this new shop run by a seamstress—an actual seamstress, they still exist—when a reflection in the window fluttered behind me. I stood there, frozen. I mean, Geneva Finch's reflection—silvery, ghostly really—gave me the strangest feeling. For a flickering instant I was sure she knew what no one else did. Years ago I had told everyone that Mira left her last manuscript with me. Easy to believe she wrote the thing and that I only edited it. And it was easy when I passed on the work, my work, through Stephanie Binks, who took a cut, and then had an assistant send it on to Thom Crystl for his signature on the contract as Mira's executor. Thom never knew, never even guessed the point of origin, although he managed to sign the worst contract imaginable, through a sister agency.

No one yet knows that the novel is mine, start to finish, although today, seeing Geneva Finch, I endured the sharp stab of what in the novel I term as "wonderment." When I looked away and then back again Geneva Finch was gone. But the look she gave me— chilling. Like someone who's figured out everything—beyond what I can begin to imagine. Like someone who won't stop working to discover whatever it is she wants to prove.

My best work: *The Green Man's Smile*. It's a marvelous title. Wonderfully enough, I owe the title to Mira. On the first day of that festival, before my panel and before she disappeared on all of us, I caught her at the building's entrance, staring at this stone mask affixed to a pillar. "That's one ugly dude," I muttered. She laughed and said, "Oh, Luisa," (she remembered my name!) "he's not ugly, he's just trying really hard to smile." In what had to be a trick of light the face appeared at that instant to grin. Maybe it was more like a grimace really. If he was trying to smile he wasn't being successful.

Later I looked up information about the mask. The Green Man, a symbol of nature. In the novel named after that strange figure I planted my own obsessions. There's not much about the color green, admittedly, and not much about the mask. It's my most autobiographical work although the ending, of course, draws exactly from what happened to Mira. My Green Man is in revolt against human selfishness.

I kept Mira Wallacz's reputation alive by writing a novel published under her name, a novel that suggested she knew how she would die. Wouldn't she have been delighted? It was more like charity than a financial arrangement on my part. I had come to Stephanie Binks with a novel manuscript at that festival when Mira met her fate. I had hoped—desperately—for representation. Stephanie made it clear that the manuscript wasn't saleable unless I added a twist—like something from Shirley Jackson. Updated. A stoning for our time. How prescient was that?

And it wasn't at all simple to rework the plot, yet my revised manuscript was ready only a few weeks after Mira's funeral. Timing, timing is everything. Ghostwriting in reverse. A way to burnish Mira's reputation with a novel that echoed the last disaster of her life. My gift to her memory. And to Stephanie, my agent. A beautiful little secret. Every single lovely review of that novel—although the novel has never yet appeared under my name—is a warm hand stretching across my heart.

During Thom Crystl's trial, Mira's posthumously published novel—my novel—went into its twenty-third printing. And now I can come forward with other "gems," bits and pieces ostensibly written by Mira. My contract—through Stephanie Binks—means that she will represent all the effluvia from the estate.

Stephanie confesses absolute faith in my judgment. In fact, I wrote the Afterword for the newest re-issue of the novel. Eventually, all will be revealed about who really wrote the novel and my own reputation, inevitably, will be changed. By then, I'll be a very rich dead woman, Stephanie tells me. She makes me laugh. Her memory—it's better than anyone's. Stephanie Binks can tell you things you don't remember that you used to be wrong about.

All you remember after a while—it's so funny—is the sensation of being wrong. And then you just remember the other sensation: the sensation of forgetting something, something on the tip of your tongue that you'll never remember. What I mean is, after a while you'll only remember there was something you forgot.

※

Acknowledgements

Sincerest thanks to Jacob Smullyan, intrepid publisher. My gratitude extends to the many writers of mysteries who have inspired
me, most prominently Agatha Christie, whose ingenious novels
lifted my spirits in difficult hours.

Thank you, dear friends, especially those who have listened to
me talk about my work: Jennifer Gilmore, Steve Belletto, Carrie
Rohman, Candace Burns, Ralph Burns, Alexis Fisher, Evan Fisher,
Marilyn Kann, Neil McElroy, Emily Schneider, and Randy Schneider.

Many thanks to my wonderful nieces and nephews and their
children and every subsequent generation.

Thank you to my marvelous son-in-law, William Burns.

To my daughters: Theodora and Cecilia, ideal readers and
artists and humorists. You and your father have given me more
happiness than I could have imagined possible.

Finally, thank you for all time past and all time to come to my
husband Eric, whose courage is beyond measure.

Lee Upton's poetry has appeared in *The New Yorker*, *The New Republic*, *Poetry*, and in many other journals as well as three editions of *Best American Poetry*. She is the author of *Tabitha, Get Up* (2024, Sagging Meniscus) and many other books of poetry, fiction, and literary criticism.

www.ingramcontent.com/pod-product-compliance
Lightning Source LLC
Chambersburg PA
CBHW031420200325
23542CB00007B/4